I0716928

Summer Stay

—Montana Beach—
Book 1

D. Allen

DN Publishing

Summer Stay
Montana Beach, Book 1
Copyright © 2018 by D. Allen
Batavia, NY

www.DavidNethBooks.com

ISBN: 978-1-945336-59-1

Subscribe to the author's newsletter for updates and exclusive content:
DavidNethBooks.com/Newsletter

Follow the author at:
www.facebook.com/DavidNethBooks

Also by D. Allen

Montana Beach
Summer Stay

Summer Job

Summer Nights

Small Town Christmas
A Christmas Reunion

A Christmas Charade

A Christmas Spark

A Christmas Song

A Christmas Departure

A Christmas Wedding

A Christmas Escape

A Christmas Renovation

Standalone
Snow After Christmas

Chapter One:
JESSIE

The best part of waking up at five in the morning is getting out on the beach for my run before the other joggers, walkers, or scavengers get out here and get in my way. Often times I don't even play music, preferring instead to listen to the waves crash along the shore. It helps me relax and prepare for the day ahead of me. The only thing on my mind is the sand under my feet and my breathing as I run my usual two-mile stretch.

It's not an easy run, that's for sure. The traction I get in the sand is quite different from what I used to get on the treadmill when I lived in the city. But the extra exertion is what I need to make this precious time count. There aren't any gyms in Montana Beach. There isn't much of anything, really.

Summer Stay

When I reach the end of the beach where it starts to get marshy, I see that the sun is sitting just on the horizon over the Atlantic Ocean. As I turn around to head back to Montana Manor, my long shadow stretches inland, interrupted only when I pass under the pier.

Grandma Ethel is sitting on the back patio with a cup of coffee watching the sunrise as I come up. I'm sweaty but energized.

"Enjoy your run, Jessie Girl?" she asks.

I nod. "The sunrise is really beautiful today."

She smiles. "It always is."

Knowing that I'm short on time, I tell Grandma, "I'll be back down soon to help you with breakfast. Just going to run up and take a shower real quick."

"Take your time, dear. I'm content right here."

Racing up the steps to the attic apartment I share with her, I head straight for the bathroom and hop in the shower.

This is the same routine I do every day. Up with the sun, run on the beach, quick shower, and then start breakfast for the guests. It's the same routine I've had for most of my life. My grandparents built Montana Manor when they first got married and have been running the small inn ever since.

It's the only place for overnight accommodations in town since the Montana Motel closed down several years ago. Well, it's the only one if you don't count the many rental houses that sit throughout the small village now that a lot of the permanent residents have moved away.

Like Montana Beach, the Manor isn't perfect. It could use a new roof, updated fixtures, and I'm sure the wiring isn't up to code. But it's home.

Braiding my wet hair, I make my way back down to the kitchen where Grandma is already frying up some eggs. I grab a pan, throw some bacon on it, and fire up the burner next to her.

"How many do we have this morning?" I ask.

"Only the Harmons. Janet said they're early-risers, so I expect them to come down anytime now."

"How long are they staying?"

"Until tomorrow night, although they still have to pay the rest of their bill. They mentioned something about paying today, but I told them they can wait until they check out, too."

"Okay." I wish Grandma wouldn't tell people that. They're our only guests and it's the middle of June, which should be the start of our busy season, but we haven't seen an uptick in guests yet. When I was a little girl the Manor used to be filled with guests from May into October. Now we're lucky if we can fill up in July.

Grandma reaches around me to grab two plates

and flips the eggs onto each of them with a spatula. "Now, if they do pay today, I want you to run to the bank to deposit some of it. The rest will have to go toward groceries."

"Did we get another reservation?" I toss the bacon onto a plate and dab away as much of the grease as I can with a paper towel.

"One couple, yes. They're arriving tomorrow. I think they may be honeymooners."

"What makes you say that?" I ask.

Grandma picks the bacon from the paper towel and arranges it on the plate while I pop some bread in the toaster.

"Their reservation came through as the Newmans, but her credit card was under a different last name."

"Then they probably are."

There isn't a lot to do in Montana Beach, but we still get a lot of honeymooners. I guess the quiet beach town is a lure to many newlyweds. Still, most of the guests we used to get are now more interested in the many activities up on North Beach, which is highly-commercialized nowadays.

The toaster pops and we hear footsteps on the stairs.

"I'll get them started with drinks," Grandma tells

me. She pulls a pitcher and a Tupperware of fruit out of the fridge and sets it on a tray with two glasses. "Can you cut this up, please?"

"I'm on it."

"Thank you, dear."

When she disappears into the dining room to greet them, I pop open the Tupperware and start cutting the fresh pineapple and cantaloupe into cubes.

"They want to eat out on the patio," Grandma tells me when she comes back in. She sets the plates on the now-empty tray.

"I can't blame them."

"Neither can I. Now hurry up with that fruit, dear, their food is getting cold."

Deciding that I've cut enough, I drop the fruit in two small bowls, pass them to Grandma, who loads everything up.

After the Harmons have been served, I return to the kitchen and pick at what's left of the bacon and finish off the extra pieces of fruit that I cut. Not the best breakfast, but I have a lot to do today.

Grandma comes in and helps me clean up. Just as I'm loading up the dishwasher, the Harmons bring in their plates.

"Oh, you didn't have to bother yourself with those!" Grandma chirps as she takes the plates from them and sets them on the counter next to me. "Did you enjoy it?"

"It was delicious, thank you," Janet says.

I look back at her and smile. "Glad you liked it."

They're an older couple who are on vacation to celebrate their recent retirement. They're friendly, but I know they only chose Montana Beach because it's quieter than North Beach or any of the other resort towns around. It would be better for business if Montana Beach wasn't viewed as a sleepy little town. Still, a guest is a guest, no matter who they are.

"Any plans for your last full day in town?" Grandma claps her hands together and brings them to her mouth like she's praying.

The Harmons turn to each other and Janet says, "I think we're going to head to the wildlife refuge and go for a walk. See if we can spot anything."

"Oh, how nice! If Cheryl's working, tell her Ethel says hello."

Mr. Harmon smiles. "Will do. Take care, now. We'll be back for dinner!"

When they're gone and the dishwasher is all loaded and running, Grandma hands me a wad of bills. "They're all paid up. Would you mind logging this into the computer before you run to the bank? I'll get started on cleaning up their room."

I take the bills and start to count it out. "Sure thing, Gram."

Montana Manor is by far the architectural jewel of Montana Beach. When my grandparents built it, they wanted it to look like a five-star stay that had a personal touch for a fraction of the cost. So the three-story Victorian building on the corner of First Street and Montana Boulevard stands out among the modest bungalows that make up most of the housing stock in town. It's situated just outside what used to be a bustling shopping district and sits right on the beach.

Originally, my grandparents lived in their own small house on Third Street, but the demands of being innkeepers became too much, especially when they had my mom, so my grandpa converted the walk-in attic to an apartment for the family, which is where I currently call home.

It's also not the best in terms of temperature control. It can be stifling hot in the summer and freezing cold in the winter. Usually it's pretty good, though, but it definitely could use some upgrades, just like the rest of the building.

Honestly, with the number of stays so low, we could probably move down into one of the bedrooms on one of the lower floors and not sacrifice too much. But we're hopeful that things will turn around.

Summer Stay

At least, Grandma is. I'm the one who faces the reality of the numbers since I'm the one who logs them into the spreadsheet on the computer. They're not good.

The corner of our large apartment living room has been serving as our office since I came back from New York. Previously, Grandma had been using a small bill-paying station in the main kitchen as the office, but I told her that it wasn't a good idea to leave our finances out in the common area where guests could see.

So with the fan blasting on me and coffee mugs, books, and other paper weights to keep everything in place, I study our financial spreadsheet in our stifling apartment. If I go out and buy $200 worth of groceries right now, we'll be operating in the red, which doesn't leave us anything to make up for the slow winter months. Even with the Newmans coming tomorrow, we don't have a lot of money to play with.

I spend the next half hour crunching numbers, trying to figure out where we can cut more expenses to save some money. Trouble is, I did this all two years ago when I first moved back home. We've cut as much out as we can.

Grandma says she doesn't need a regular salary thanks to the stash of savings that Grandpa left her when he died. I'm already paying myself under the table at a rate lower than minimum, and I'm considering cutting that as well. Since we're living here, we don't need to pay for our own housing costs, but we do need to live.

We don't even have a lot of amenities to offer our guests. We took the TVs out of each room and cut out cable in favor of a couple streaming apps for the TV in the common living room. Sure, we have the pool, but when you stay at a beach house, you kind of expect a pool. Losing that would take away one of our selling points for guests. And of course there's the beach, but people expect more than that nowadays.

Unless we want to be known as the ones who don't leave their guests toilet paper, we're fresh out of options for cutting costs.

Frustrated, I turn off the computer, cut off the power to the fan, grab the money from the Harmons, and head downstairs. Grandma's throwing a load of towels in the washer in the small closet off the kitchen.

"Just wanted to let you know that I'm heading out now," I tell her.

"Oh good, you didn't leave yet. Did you make a grocery list?"

Reaching behind my blonde hair to scratch my neck, I say, "Uh, no. I'm only picking up a few things." Since that's all we can afford...

"Well, I think we should get the Newmans a little something for when they arrive. Wouldn't that be special? They are newlyweds, after all."

"A gift? Like what?"

Grandma waves her fingers at me and returns to loading the washer. "Anything you can find. Think of it as a wedding present."

"We don't know they're newlyweds for sure."

"Well, they're on vacation either way."

I nod. "Right. Well, I'll see what I can find."

"Thank you, dear!"

As I run my errands, I consider the best way to tell Grandma how bad things are for us, but every time I try to start the conversation in my head, it always ends with her disappointed look and a pointed, "Oh. Okay."

Montana Manor was her and Grandpa's dream. It's a part of him that still lives on even after his death. It's probably why Grandma doesn't see the need to upgrade the house too much. She'd see it as undoing the work he's done.

Everything in town is within walking distance, so it doesn't take me long to finish my errands. After I've unloaded the groceries, I grab a vase from the cupboard above the fridge and start filling it with water.

"Ooo," Grandma coos when she sees the flowers on the counter. "Is this what you got for the Newmans?"

"Yeah. I figured it was something nice without

going too overboard." It didn't hurt that they were only ten bucks, too.

Grandma brings them to her nose and sniffs. "They're pretty. Make sure to put them where they can get plenty of light until they arrive."

"Yes, Gram."

"Oh, and someone called while you were out. Could you check that? I want to get started on the flower garden out front."

"Sure, who was it? Do you know?"

"No idea, but if it's a potential guest it's probably better to call them soon and get them to commit to a stay before they go somewhere else."

See, Grandma's not completely ignorant to the issues with the Manor. She just doesn't ever talk about them.

Once I've put the flowers in the dining room window overlooking the patio and the beach, I go to the little bill-paying station in the corner of the kitchen. It may have been downgraded from the official office for the Manor, but we still use it to take calls and check people in.

I hit play on the answering machine and a gruff man's voice says, "Hi, I'm trying to reach Jessica Ray. Jessica, my name's Jack Tyson and I just wanted to talk to you about the future of Montana Manor. Give me a call back when you get a chance—"

"Oh good, you got my message," the same voice says from behind me.

I jump at the sound of his voice, just as the automated machine voice says, "End of new messages."

"Are you Jessica Ray?" He looks to be about my age, maybe a little older, but no more than thirty-five. Still, the black business suit he's wearing makes him look like he's older than he probably is. He shifts a black folder to his left hand as he steps forward to shake my hand.

"Jessie," I correct. "You must be Jack Tyson."

He nods. "Yes, ma'am. I met your grandmother outside. She said I could come in."

"Oh sure, yeah." I motion through the doorway to the living room. "Here, let's sit down. Do you want anything? Water? Coffee? Anything?"

"No thanks, I'm all set."

I lead him into the next room and take a seat in an oversized chair. The room is designed for comfort, so when he sits down, he falls back further than he expects.

"Whoa." He laughs. "Didn't think it'd eat me."

I grin and wait for him to reposition himself on the edge of the couch.

He sets the folder on the coffee table, intertwines his fingers and asks, "How are things going?"

I shrug and maintain my smile, not sure what he means. "They're fine."

"Everything's going well with the business and everything?"

Nodding, I say, "Yeah, we're chugging along."

"So you're struggling?"

"I didn't say that," I shoot back.

"Miss Ray, I didn't mean for it to sound like an attack. I apologize for that. What I mean is, the village of Montana Beach has seen a steady drop in population over the last few years. Along with the people, the businesses have been disappearing as well. Now that a lot of the stores and restaurants are closed, there isn't a lot for tourists to do here —"

I hold up my hand to stop him. "What's your point?"

"Montana Manor has become iconic to the village," he says. "Not necessarily because of its architectural design, which is unconventional for this area, but because of its proximity to the ocean, state parks, and North Beach."

"The architectural design is '*unconventional*'?" I'm offended on behalf of my grandfather.

"It's beautiful, don't get me wrong, but it doesn't really fit in with the style people think of when they imagine a relaxing beach vacation."

"What are you getting at?"

"I would like to discuss with you—and your grandmother—what it would cost to take the Manor off your hands."

My brow furrows. "You mean you want to buy it?"

He nods. "Absolutely. Real estate in North Beach is getting increasingly expensive and I believe that Montana Beach is the next hotspot."

"Hmm." It's intriguing. If we didn't own the Manor, we wouldn't have to pay for its upgrades and we may be able to still manage it. This might be the answer to our financial issues and would ensure that the building is maintained the way that it should be.

Mr. Tyson smiles. "I can see you're considering it."

"Well, I'd need more details first. How much are you offering? What does the future look like if this went through? Would we still manage it? Would you hire new staff? Would we have to move out of the apartment upstairs?"

Mr. Tyson's smile fades and he opens the folder. "Well, I had something specific in mind."

He hands me the folder and I see a rendering for a glass-faced hotel tower with several balconies angled toward the ocean. It still doesn't hit me what it is until I notice the other landmarks by the street.

"You want to *tear down* the Manor?"

"We'd pay you full market value."

I set the folder on the coffee table and shake my head. "No."

"Miss Ray, this building is outdated. It's past its prime. By working with me, you're ensuring that thousands of families will be able to enjoy everything Montana Beach has to offer for generations to come."

"What about the generations of families that have already enjoyed the Manor? What about the historic value of it? What about the family-owned business you'll be shutting down for an overbuilt hotel that doesn't offer the same personal touch that we can?"

Montana Beach is my home. I don't want to see it become a smaller version of North Beach.

He taps the folder. "I can leave this here with you to think about."

I pick it up and hand it to him. "No, there's nothing to think about. We're not selling. Thank you, Mr. Tyson."

When I stand, he hesitates, but follows suit. I lead him to the door, but before he leaves, he hands me a business card and says, "Think about it."

"Goodbye, Mr. Tyson."

Finally, he leaves just as another man approaches. The newcomer is wearing a maroon T-shirt that's soaked with sweat. It doesn't help that he's in a dark pair of jeans and has a large bag slung over his shoulder.

"Are you the one I talk to about getting a room?" he asks with a smile. When he steps inside, he removes his sunglasses.

"We don't take walk-ins," I tell him with the edge still present from Mr. Tyson. The no walk-ins policy came during our prime, as Mr. Tyson called it. When we were almost always booked to capacity.

"Oh," he looks disappointed. "Is there anywhere else in town you can point me to? Or maybe make the exception this one time?"

I sigh, remembering how bad our finances are. "Yeah, I suppose. Come in. We should be able to get you into a room."

He steps inside and drops his bag by the door. "Thank you, so much." He offers his hand. "I'm Mason."

Chapter Two:
MASON

With the stream of sunlight escaping through the blinds, I can see tiny flecks of dust floating in the air. The sound of the waves on the beach remind me where I am. Some kind of inn in Montana Beach. I've never heard of it or the town, but it seems like a nice enough place to relax for the next month. It could be just what I need.

I sit up in bed and wipe the sleep out of my eyes. The room isn't huge, but it's nice. Hardwood floors, a comfortable bed, and French doors that open to a shared patio. There's a Jack and Jill bathroom here too, but I don't think anyone's in the other room.

Actually, I don't think there are any other guests at the inn but me. Then again, I've been sleeping basically since I arrived. Driving eleven hours straight through from New York City will do that to you. Especially when you forget to consider the fact that you're driving south in the summertime. Talk about hot. I was glad to get out of those jeans when I finally got to the room.

I open the French doors and step through to enjoy the beach view. The balcony is shared with the same room on the other end of the bathroom, which means I have it completely to myself.

Judging from the height of the sun and the number of the people on the beach, I'd say it's at least late morning, if not already noon. Guess I better get going to see if they're still serving that breakfast Jessie told me about yesterday. She's cute and I'd love the chance to see her again.

After showering and changing into some weather-appropriate clothes, I head downstairs to the dining room, which is eerily quiet. In the kitchen, Jessie is emptying the dishwasher and Ethel is sitting on a stool at the counter reading a newspaper.

"Oh, good morning sleepy-head!" Ethel says with a smile.

"Is it still morning?" I ask.

"You're in Montana Beach! Time doesn't matter!" Jessie snickers from across the counter.

"Well, whatever time it is, I could use something to

eat. I take it it's too late for breakfast?"

"We had breakfast ready at nine, when you said you'd be up," Jessie tells me.

I feel a twinge of guilt, imagining both of them getting up and waiting for me to join them.

"Jessie, don't be rude," Ethel scolds. "We haven't had a guest *this* good-looking in a while."

"What about the other guests?" I ask.

Ethel gets up and pats my cheek gently. "It's just you for now, sweetie. We have another couple coming today, but otherwise, you get this whole house to yourself. How's that sound for a vacation?"

"Oh. Okay." My stomach grumbles loudly.

Jessie closes up the dishwasher and turns to me. "Dinner will be at six. That is, if you'll be joining us."

I feel my face flush. Luckily, I already have some color in my cheeks, so it hides it well. "Yes, I'll make sure I'm here."

"Oh good!" Ethel exclaims. "Well, unfortunately we don't have anything in the way of a meal prepared. We have a few snacks in the cupboard, but if you're looking for something more filling, you may need to go somewhere in town."

"Okay, sure. Where's the best place to go?"

"First Street Diner," Jessie replies. "It's about the only place still open."

"Oh, don't listen to her." Ethel waves Jessie off. "There's also the Nine and they make subs at the gas station on the edge of town."

"Great suggestions, Gram," she says with sarcasm.

"Well, either way, the First Street Diner is good," Ethel tells me. "If you see Marsha, make sure you tell her I said hello."

I nod and smile. "Will do. Thank you both."

The walk to the diner doesn't take long. I didn't really pay attention on my drive in yesterday, but now I see that this town isn't that big. I could probably walk all the streets in the village in a single day and still have time left to go to the beach.

To my surprise, though, there's a lot of people in the diner.

"Sit anywhere, hun," the waitress calls from behind the breakfast counter.

I find a free spot at the corner of the breakfast bar. The menu has the standard diner fare, but I'm after breakfast, which they serve all day.

The waitress comes over with a pot of coffee in her hand and a pen tucked behind her ear. "Well, you're new. I'm Marsha, what's your name?"

"Mason." I turn over the mug set by the silverware and hold it out for her. "Thanks."

"Well, Mason, what can I get for you?"

I skim the menu. "The, uh, number two special." Bacon, sausage, hash browns, and eggs. Exactly what I need on my first day of vacation.

"I'll get that right in for you," she tells me and disappears to the back.

As I sip my coffee, I scan some of the people here. Most of them are older. There are a few younger people and one family, but they seem to be the exception. That's probably how Marsha picked up on the fact that I'm new right away.

"So Mason, what brings you to our neck of the woods?" Marsha asks me as she refills someone else's coffee at the other end of the breakfast bar.

"Just wanted to unplug for a little bit. This seemed like the perfect place."

"Unplug from what?"

"Life in New York."

"Ooo, the big city!" Excitement flashes in Marsha's eyes. "What's that like?"

"Busy." I grin. "I have kind of a big decision to make—a *really* big decision, actually, and I thought I'd take a couple weeks off to consider it. For whatever reason, I decided to stop in Montana Beach."

"Well, I'm glad you did. You staying in town?"

I nod. "At the—"

"Montana Manor." She says with a smile. "Mm-hmm. It's one of the few places in Montana Beach that really draws in guests anymore. How long you staying?"

"Four weeks," I say.

"Wow, mighty long vacation."

"Yeah. My dad's my boss, though, so I have a little leeway."

"Working with family can be trouble, but Ethel and Jessie seem to manage it just fine. They've kept that place running for a long time."

"It seems like a nice place. Ethel said to tell you hi, by the way."

Marsha laughs. "Oh, I'm sure she did. Ethel and I go back a bit. Both opened up businesses at the same time, back when Montana Beach was a bubbling tourist town. Of course, that was before North Beach became as big as it is today."

I lean forward a bit. "Wait a minute, you own this place?"

"Mm-hmm, haven't missed a day in thirty years." She shrugs. "Well, there have been a *few* days. I have three kids, who all moved away, but this place has been with me for a long time."

"Wow, that's great."

"I just hope I don't have to close it down."

A few other people at the bar glance up in her direction with worried looks.

"Why would you have to close it down?" I ask.

"Look around." She waves out the window. "This place is a ghost town compared to what it used to be. It's sad to have watched all of those wonderful little shops close down. For a while it seemed like this town was doomed to fail. Every time a new store opened, it was gone within six months."

"Oh, I'm sorry to hear that."

She pats the counter in front of me. "You're sweet. I'm glad you're here. Make sure you treat those girls well at the Manor, you got that?"

"Yes, ma'am."

Marsha grabs my plate from the window to the kitchen and sets it in front of me. "You said you're sticking around here for a bit?"

"Yes, ma'am."

"Good. I hope I'll see you again soon, then. Enjoy."

On the walk back to the Manor, I notice the empty storefronts I missed before. It's not hard to picture the different businesses that once existed in these forgotten spaces. Bakeries, hair salons, clothing stores, restaurants.

It makes me wonder why these people chose to stay. Wouldn't they want to live somewhere with more going on? At the very least, wouldn't they want to get out of a town that's so bleak?

Summer Stay

As I cross Montana Boulevard to the Manor, I catch sight of the beach. The crowd seems to have dispersed, maybe because of the wind, which has picked up strength since I left. Either way, the view is beautiful. It's exactly what I was looking for: relaxation.

Racing up to my room, I notice the bed's been made and my bag set on top of the dresser next to a row of books in place of a TV. I won't miss it. Who would want to watch TV with a view like this?

I quickly unpack my bag into the drawers until I get to my swim trunks and change into them. Grabbing a beach towel from the bathroom, I head downstairs and out toward the back door.

"You're not going on the beach, are you?" Ethel calls to me when my hand is on the doorknob in the dining room. She has a watering can in her hand and is tending to the various plants throughout the house.

I glance down at my attire. "That was my plan."

"Oh no. It's too windy for that. You'll get sand blowing everywhere, you won't enjoy it. Go tomorrow."

"Oh, well, I think I'll be fi —"

"No, no." She pats my bare arm and her eyes take a long time to meet mine as she glances at my body. "Go tomorrow. If you really want to enjoy the sunshine, we have the pool. The Newmans won't be here until after dinner, so it's all yours for today."

"Uh, okay. Sure. That's what I'll do then." I was really hoping to hit the beach, but I guess she has a point about the sand.

She offers me another smile and turns back to the plants inside. When I've got the door open, she calls to me again.

"Oh, Mason."

"Yeah?"

"My granddaughter and I will be in and out doing odds and ends. Please, don't let us bother you. If either of us are in the way, just let us know."

"Oh, I'm sure it won't be a problem." I quickly walk through the door to the patio to avoid further interruption from the start of my relaxation.

The pool is crystal clear. I dip my toes in to test the temperature. It's not too bad. First, though, I just want to lie in the sun. I haven't had a vacation like this since spring break my senior year of college.

Claiming one of the lounge chairs around the pool as my own, I lay my towel down, slip on my sunglasses, and kick back, letting the heat waves soak into my skin.

With the sound of the ocean and the seagulls in the air, it's very relaxing. Almost too relaxing. I can't let myself fall asleep in the sun, because that would ruin my whole trip—not to mention give me uneven tan lines. Oh, the horror!

Summer Stay

After laying there for a long while, I decide to get up to cool off in the pool when I hear the door open from the house. Squinting behind my sunglasses, I see Jessie with a squeegee and bucket. She dunks the end in the bucket and raises it to the window. After the window is thoroughly soaked, she takes one sweep with the skimmer and it's left perfectly clear.

"Very nice," I say.

She jumps and clutches at her chest. "You scared the crap out of me!"

I smile and sit up. "Sorry."

She turns back to the window. "I just have these few and then I'll be out of your way."

"No, it's okay. Do you want any help?"

"I've got it. You're the guest. Have you tried out the pool?"

"Not yet." I get up and head over to the pool steps, still watching Jessie, but trying not to make it obvious.

The water is chilly at first, but it feels nice on my sun kissed skin. I step in until the water's up to my waist and wade through the water to Jessie's side, resting my arms against the concrete patio.

She's up on her tiptoes over the large pool pump. The squeegee is raised high above her head as she tries to wipe at a cobwebbed window above the pump.

"You sure you don't need my reach?"

"I can get it."

Hauling myself out of the water, I go over to her and reach for the squeegee.

"Mind if I try? I know you said you've got it, and I believe you, but I've never cleaned a window before and I'd just love the opportunity." I grin to show I'm joking.

She rolls her eyes with a smirk and passes it to me.

I have to stretch onto my toes too, but I don't have to raise the squeegee as high, which gives me more strength to brush away the cobwebs and clear off the window.

With the mess gone, I pass it back to her and say, "Okay, you can finish up now."

"Oh, you don't want to help me with the rest?"

"Nah." I step back into the water. "I have my own list of things to do today: work on my tan, relax in the pool, forget about my troubles. It's my whole Hakuna Matata motto for this trip."

She laughs. "Oh, well I wouldn't want to interrupt your busy schedule! I'll leave you to it."

"You could join me," I add quickly. "Unless you prefer washing windows to my jam-packed schedule. Both equally important, I might add."

Jessie picks up the bucket. "I don't think so."

"I'm serious, you know. I'd like to take you out sometime."

Her smile fades. "Uh, no. I don't really have the money to go anywhere."

"My treat."

She shakes her head. "I couldn't let you do that."

"We could hang out here, then. Whatever you want to do."

"No, I've been really busy and I don't really have the time to go out."

I give her a tight smile, taking the hint. "Okay. Maybe some other time, then."

Her eyes linger on me a moment and then she disappears back inside the house.

Chapter Three:
JESSIE

I grab my headphones and quietly make my way down the stairs to the beach. The sun's rays are just starting to peek up over the horizon. By time I come back, it'll be out in full force.

I'm in such a hurry to get outside that I collide into Mason on my way to the door.

"Oh!" I exclaim.

"Sorry!"

We both stumble backward away from each other and I clutch at my chest to catch my breath.

"You scared the crap out of me!" I whisper-shout in the quiet house. The last thing I need is to wake the Newmans on their first morning here.

"You've said that before," he says with a chuckle. "I

was just about to go for a sunrise walk. Want to come?"

He's in a pair of gym shorts and a blue tank top. I hate to admit it, but he looks good. But I'm glad to see his hair is matted and standing on end. At least I don't look like a *total* slob next to him in my worn gym clothes and my blonde hair in a messy bun.

"Oh, I was actually just going to go for a run on the beach," I reply.

"Mind if I come?"

I glance outside at the rising sun and then back at Mason. It's getting late. I need to get going soon so I can be back in time to make breakfast. But if he thinks this is another way he can get me involved with some summer fling, then he's out of his fricken mind.

"Uh, sure. If you can keep up."

He smirks. "Oh, I can keep up."

I motion to his outfit. "I don't know if I can wait for you to change, though. I have a lot of stuff to do this morning."

He tugs at his shirt. "Oh, this? I'll be fine. I'll just have to borrow the washer at some point."

"Okay. Let's get going, then." I lead him out to the beach and start walking briskly as I untangle my headphones. It's brighter than it usually is when I start running. I've already wasted a lot of time chitchatting with Mason. Not to mention the fact that I overslept.

"So how far do you run?"

Pointing toward the pier, I say, "About a mile past that. I'm not sure how far it is exactly." I tuck my phone in my pocket, slip in my earbuds, and take off.

Even with the music in my ears, I can hear Mason's footsteps not far behind me. He keeps up for about a song and a half and then he starts to fall back.

When I reach the point where I turn around, he's still a little ways off and when I pass him, he's red in the face and sweaty. It makes me smile. I press on until I reach the back deck of the Manor. Looking down the beach, I see he's just coming out from under the pier, so I head inside.

I don't have time to run up and shower. Grandma's already in the kitchen pulling biscuits out of the oven.

"There you are!" She hands me the spatula. "Finish up these eggs, will you? The Newmans said they're going to be up early today. Have you heard from Mr. Wagner?"

Setting my headphones on the counter, I turn to the frying pan and flip the eggs.

"Mason? Yeah, he went for a run with me. He's still out there."

Grandma's face stretches into a wide grin. "Oh! I didn't realize you two were getting so cozy with one another. I suppose it makes sense. You're about the same age and—"

"Grandma—"

"—you're both so good-looking, you'd make the perfect couple. Oh, I could just picture—"

"Grandma—"

"—how cute your kids would be! Oh, and you've been so lonely. It would really be a delight to see you happy again!"

"Grandma, we're not together!" I turn off the burner and transfer the eggs to three clean plates.

"Well, naturally. Not yet, at least. He's only been here a day! I know you've been lonely, dear, but I wouldn't say you were *desperate*. But you should still keep an open mind—"

She stops as soon as Mason walks through the door, sweating and huffing. He takes a seat on the barstool at the counter and wipes the sweat from his forehead.

"Oh, look at you, dear." Grandma giggles. "Bet you thought you could keep up with my Jessie Girl, huh?"

I set the plates on the counter and grab a glass from the cupboard to pour him some water.

He gulps it down quickly and looks at me through ragged breaths. "You...do that...*every* morning?"

I smile and pull the butter out of the fridge. "Yup.

You kept up for a while, though."

He presses the cold glass to his cheek. "No, I thought I was a pretty good runner, but *that* was…I don't know."

"Running in sand takes more out of you," I tell him to cut him some slack.

"Jessie's always been athletic," Grandma adds. She pulls out several glasses from the cupboard and gathers everything on a tray to take to the dining room.

"I can see that," Mason says.

Snatching a few paper towels off the roll, I pass them to him. "It's the only way I really get to enjoy the beach. The rest of the time I'm working on things here."

He wipes away the sweat from his face until it hits him that we're preparing breakfast for everyone. "Oh, I'm sorry. What can I do to help?"

Grandma smacks his leg with a wooden spoon and says, "You can go clean up and make yourself presentable for our new guests. They'll be down any minute, so hurry up!"

"Yes, ma'am."

When he gets up, she smacks his butt with the spoon and adds, "Go on!"

I laugh to myself as I roll my eyes. I grab the pitcher of orange juice from the fridge to carry out to the table. I wish I could unsee what I just saw, but it shouldn't come as a surprise. Grandma's always embarrassing when our guests are younger men. Maybe that's why we don't have too many of them.

"You know, Jessie Girl, if I were your age, I'd jump on him the moment I had the chance," she says.

I grin. "Oh yeah? And then what? He'll go home and I'll be stuck here."

"Even so, at least you'll have a good time while he's here." She looks back to where Mason disappeared up the stairs and adds, "Mmm, and I bet he'd be a *really* good time."

"Grandma!"

The Newmans come down before she can retort. Since Grandma checked them in, this is the first time I'm seeing them. She was right, they are newlyweds. And young ones, at that. Probably ten years younger than me. Gosh, that makes me feel so old and dried up. Maybe Grandma has a point and I should just take advantage of the opportunities I have now before they're gone.

"How'd you two sleep?" Grandma asks.

"Good," Mrs. Newman says. She's a tiny little girl with long blonde hair and cut off jean shorts. She can't be any more than twenty. Could even be eighteen or nineteen.

"Everything was very comfortable," her husband

adds. He has curly brown hair that half covers the zit on his forehead. I wonder if they both just graduated high school.

"Well, you know every room is insulated for privacy, so don't worry about—"

"Grandma!" I shout.

The newlyweds laugh and Grandma just shrugs.

"Just in case they were worried," she says innocently.

"Sorry for that," I tell them.

They both turn red and laugh.

Mason comes down and quickly takes the third open place at the table.

"If you folks need anything else, please let me or my granddaughter know," Grandma tells the room. "Also, please keep us posted on your dinner plans so we know how many people to expect to feed."

Mr. Newman raises his hand for a second before wiping his mouth. "We actually have dinner plans in North Beach. We probably won't be back until late."

Grandma nods. "Oh, how lovely. Well, I hope you two have a splendid evening. Mr. Wagner?"

"Oh please, call me Mason. And as far as I know, I'll be here. Wouldn't miss it."

Grandma turns to me and winks. "I'm sure you wouldn't."

"How long have you been here?" the young Mrs. Newman asks Mason.

I take that as my cue to head back into the kitchen and get a jump on the dishes. The sooner I can get these cleaned up, the sooner I can get in the shower and wash the sweat off from my run. I usually don't like to wait this long, but guests come first.

By the time I'm done scrubbing away the large pans in the sink, Grandma starts bringing in the plates from the dining room.

"Well, the Newmans are off to North Beach," she says with a defeated tone.

"Yeah, I heard that. But, at least they're staying here. That has to count for something." I take the dishes from her and rinse them off in the sink before loading them in the dishwasher.

"And we still have Mr. Wagner—I mean, Mason." She pokes my side and grins.

"What?"

"Nothing." She grabs a brillo pad and starts scrubbing at the stove. Grandma has always had an obsession with keeping the Manor spotless from top to bottom.

Mason comes in from the dining room and says, "Okay, you wouldn't let me help you make breakfast, at least let me help with the cleanup."

"Sure, do you want to wipe down the table in the dining room?" I ask before Grandma can turn him down. Hey, even if he is on vacation, he's the one who offered to help.

"Actually, Mason, I want to get started on my planters in the upstairs windows," Grandma says. "Would you mind taking over for me here? Some of these spots need a little extra elbow grease."

He takes the brillo pad from her and steps over to the stove. "Sure, not a problem."

I give Grandma a look as she disappears out of the room. Guess she'd rather fix me up with someone than make sure our guests are completely relaxed.

Mason and I are both quiet as I finish loading the dishwasher. By the time I hit 'Start,' Mason's still working at a blemish on the stove. I don't want to just leave him here. It's not his job and it's not his house. But, he's also doing a better job at it than I would.

"So, uh, Mason," I start, "what do you do for a living?" Wow, that was so natural. Not.

"I'm kind of sort of between jobs now. Not unemployed or anything, but I have some options to consider that will change things."

"Like what?"

"Work stuff. I just thought I'd take some time to relax before I really decided."

Summer Stay

Message received. He doesn't want to talk about it. A part of me wants to ask how he's paying to stay here for a month if he's not working, but I know that'd be rude, so I don't say anything.

"What about you?" He wipes the stove off with a wet paper towel. "How long have you been working with your grandma?"

"Well, with the exception of a five-year stint up north, I've been here my whole life. My grandma and grandpa started this place and have lived here since before I was born. I moved back to help after Grandpa died."

"What about your parents?"

"They're divorced and my mom isn't interested in the Manor, so I was the only one who could step in to prevent my grandma's whole world from being ripped out from under her."

"Where did you live up north?"

The Old Car Horn ringtone blares loudly from my phone on the counter.

"That's me," I tell him.

When I answer it, I hear Jack Tyson's voice on the other end.

"Miss Ray, how are you today?"

"I'm doing well, Mr. Tyson. How can I help you? Are you calling to reserve a room?"

"All of them, actually," he says. "I was just wondering if you've considered the offer I made you the other day."

"I haven't changed my mind. We're not selling."

"Miss Ray, I urge you not to make this decision in haste."

"I'm not. Not only is the Manor our livelihood, it's our home. We're not selling." Maybe he'll get it the second time.

"Okay, well, keep in mind that if you don't sell now on terms we can agree on, I'll have no choice but to go directly to the village board and ask them to take the property via eminent domain."

I narrow my eyes and study the messy counter while I consider what he's saying. "What does that mean, exactly?"

"It means that whether or not you decide to sell, the village can take the property from you and sell it to me for my development. One way or another, my hotel will be built."

"Why are you so intent on destroying my home?" I don't even care that Mason's hearing this. I just can't let Mr. Tyson think he's got me cornered. "If you get rid of the Manor, you might as well say goodbye to the charm that still attracts people to Montana Beach."

"*Are* people still attracted to Montana Beach?

Based on the numbers of tourist traffic I obtained from the feasibility study I had done, the numbers don't hold a candle to other similarly-sized towns. The charm of Montana Beach is gone. Nobody's staying at Montana Manor anymore because it's old and outdated. With a new state-of-the-art resort, that would change. I'm sure the village would love to have a piece of the tourism pie again. Capitalize on what's drawing people to North Beach."

"And what says visitors from North Beach aren't staying with us? We have a couple with us now who are spending the whole day in North Beach. Obviously, there was something alluring about our 'old and outdated' inn."

"Miss Ray, this isn't an attack on you or your grandmother. This is simply a business deal that you can benefit from greatly if you're open to discussion."

"Well, we're not. Goodbye, Mr. Tyson." I toss my phone on the counter after I hang up and rub my face in my hands.

"Do you want me to go?" Mason asks softly from across the room. He's drying his hands with a dish towel.

I cross my arms and sigh. "No, you're fine. It's just a jerk who thinks he can walk all over me and my grandma."

"Well, from what I heard, you stood your ground."

He leans against the counter across from me.

"It won't do any good, though."

"Why's that? What does he want?"

I'm sure he heard part of it, so what does it matter if I tell him the whole thing? "He wants to buy the Manor from us to tear it down and build a resort hotel. Basically, he wants to turn Montana Beach into North Beach Junior."

Mason shakes his head. "I don't think he can do that."

"I guess he can. Apparently, he doesn't even need our approval to take the Manor from us. The village can intervene and take it with eminent domain."

"Oh."

"Yeah. And it's not like we can say that this is a successful business because lately it hasn't been. If it weren't for you showing up unannounced, we would have been serving cereal for breakfast."

"I'm sure you'll get more people."

I shake my head. "Not since I've been back. Each summer there's fewer people. I just don't know how long we can keep trudging along like this."

"Maybe you should consider his offer," he suggests.

"Absolutely not. My grandpa built this place. It was his and Grandma's dream. I can't let that die. We used to be turning people away. Now it seems like we're begging them to stay."

"Well, that's a different problem to consider," he says. "But as far as saving the building itself, maybe you should go to the mayor or someone at the village directly and pitch your case. Tell them what you just told me and maybe they won't even consider this guy's offer."

I nod slowly. The mayor is a friend of Grandma's. She knows how much my family's brought to the community. How hard my grandparents worked to build this business.

"You know, that's not a bad idea," I admit.

"Oh, hello Jessie. Come on in," Patty tells me from her office at the village hall above one of the many empty storefronts on First Street.

I take a seat in the cold metal chair across from her desk. It's a momentary relief in the stifling hot room. Her office is small and feels boxy thanks to the floor to ceiling paneling throughout. An effort in the 80s to "freshen up" the old buildings. Yuck. There's a tall filing cabinet tucked in the corner and other than her desk and the chair I'm sitting in, there isn't room for much else.

"I've never been up here," I tell her. "The view down the street is really something."

Through the window behind Patty's desk there's a nice view of the ocean. From the window in the narrow hallway outside, Montana Beach's little downtown area is on full display in the afternoon sun.

"Yeah, it's certainly charming," she says. "The lack of proper AC and the questionable wiring kind of overrules that, though. We're considering alternative options for the village hall."

"It just needs some TLC."

She smiles. "You sound just like your grandmother. Unfortunately, the care that this building requires is beyond our financial scope. A lot of things are out of our reach financially these days."

"Oh." In the pit of my stomach, I have a sinking feeling that I'm not going to walk out of here with the answer I want.

"You said on the phone you wanted to talk to me about the future of Montana Manor?"

"Yes, exactly."

After my conversation with Mason yesterday, I called the village office to schedule a meeting with Patty Moore, the village mayor. Since it's such a small town, being mayor isn't her full-time job, so she was working. We scheduled our meeting for tonight, when she was home, though.

"Well, what seems to be on your mind?"

"I was approached by someone who said he was interested in buying the Manor from me and my grandma."

Patty nods slowly. "Your grandmother has owned the Manor for a very long time."

"I know. But, to be quite honest, we could use the money."

"Can't we all?"

"Unfortunately," I continue, "this man isn't interested in just taking over operations of the Manor. He wants to tear it down to build a resort hotel."

"Yes, it is unfortunate."

"You know about it?" I ask.

"The plans Mr. Tyson has submitted have come across my desk in preparation for our zoning board meeting. The height of the proposed building is in question. Some wonder whether it would distort the historic image of the village."

A smile spreads across my face. The rendering I saw looked completely out of place from the rest of the buildings. There's no way it would be approved if they take historic value into account.

"Oh, so there's a chance he wouldn't even be able to build it?"

Patty rocks her head back and forth. "Well, I'm not sure."

"He called me yesterday to tell me that the village can take it away without our permission. Is that true?"

"Yes, technically. It's a long and expensive process, but if a municipality wants a property, they can get it."

"But that's not fair! We've been here for fifty years! We're iconic to Montana Beach now."

"I know, but as you said it yourself, we could all use more money. The village is no exception. Population is declining and so is the sales tax revenue. We're getting desperate to bring new revenue streams into the village."

"So you're going to sacrifice one of the last remaining businesses for a project that doesn't fit in with the rest of the community?"

"I understand where you're coming from, Jessie, and believe me when I say that I don't want to see the Manor disappear either, but it's the project that's being proposed at the moment. It could save our village from extinction."

"What do you mean 'extinction'?"

She sighs. "There's been talks about the village dissolving."

"So what would happen to the town? Who would be in charge of it?"

"We'd probably be absorbed by North Beach, which has been continuously expanding its city limits."

"But that would mean that a project like Mr.

Tyson's would have no problem being passed!"

The shores of North Beach are filled with tall bland concrete buildings built by one developer after another to take advantage of the number of people flocking there each year. Montana Beach has always been the quieter alternative to that. The slower pace used to be a draw to travelers. Now it seems like it's a detriment to the community.

"I know," Patty says. "But if we can't get more money in our hands, that may be our only option. I'm sorry, Jessie, but we need to seriously consider Mr. Tyson's proposal."

Chapter Four:
MASON

"Hey, how'd it go?" I ask Jessie when she comes through the door.

I've been sitting on the couch in the living room trying to dive in to the Manor's copy of *Murder on the Orient Express*. Unfortunately, Ethel's constant interruptions to ask if I need anything or to suggest I read outside have prevented me from getting more than five pages in.

Jessie scowls at me as she slams the door behind her. She starts toward me with her finger pointed at me, but Ethel comes through the door.

"Sweetie, what are you slamming doors for? Mason is trying to read!"

I raise my eyebrows and tuck one of the Manor's

business cards in between the pages and set the book down.

"Nothing," Jessie tells her, trying to play off her intent to yell. "Sorry."

"Well, just be careful next time," Ethel says. "Would you mind checking the pool filter? The pump's been running pretty loud all morning." Turning to me, she adds, "We'll be out of your hair shortly, dear."

"No, it's okay. My fault for reading inside on a nice day like this anyway."

When Ethel disappears in the kitchen, Jessie escapes to the patio. After giving her a moment, I decide to follow her.

Outside, she has the cover off for the pool system that's situated near the house. The large filters are covered in thick coats of green grime and she mutters, "Yeah, that'll do it."

"Need some help?" I ask.

She jumps. "Oh, it's you. No, I'm fine. I just need to hose these down." Getting up, she moves to the side of the house, opens a panel on the side of the building and flips a switch that shuts off the pump.

"Mind if I just sit here anyway?" I ask.

She turns and puts her hands on her hips. "Why don't you just say what you want to say?"

I stare down at my bare feet burning on the hot

concrete. "Okay, how did it go with the mayor? Not well, I'm assuming."

Jessie turns back to the filter, unhooks something at the bottom, and lifts the two-foot cylinder from its place. "She basically told me that if Mr. Tyson's willing to pay, there's nothing we can do."

"Oh."

"Yeah." She sets the filter down on the edge of the concrete where the fence separates the patio and the sand. "And I don't know how I'm going to tell my grandma about it. This place was her whole life. I can't just do nothing."

"So don't." I reach for the hose coiled up on the holder that's bolted to the wall.

Jessie uncoils it as I step away to stretch it out. "Well, I'm fresh out of options right now. We can't really spend much more on advertising and unless we get more people in here—" She breaks off and shakes her head. She walks up and takes the end of the hose from me. "Sorry. I shouldn't be whining to you. You're on vacation."

"No, it's okay. I asked. But I think you're wrong."

She hooks an eyebrow. "About what?"

"That there's nothing else you can do."

"Do *you* have any ideas?"

"I might."

"Like what?"

"You could—"

Ethel pokes her head out of the back door. "Mason, dear, you don't have to help Jessie with that. If you want to use the pool, she can change the filters later."

"We're just talking." I tell her with a wave.

She grins. "Ooooh, I see. Well then, carry on."

When she's gone, Jessie rolls her eyes. "Could she be any more obvious?"

I laugh. "Probably, I'm sure."

"Anyway, we probably shouldn't talk about the Manor here. I don't want her to overhear."

"We could go to dinner. I'm sure your grandma would love that." I wouldn't mind it, either.

Jessie studies me as she considers. "Okay, sure. But only to discuss…what we were just talking about. Don't get any ideas."

I put up my right hand. "Scout's honor."

She smiles. "Good. Now get out of here and let me work."

"Jessie Girl!" Marsha exclaims when we step into the diner. She hugs her tight and then looks over at me. "Oh, I see you're showing this young man around."

Jessie stifles a smile. "It's just dinner."

"Oh, right," Marsha says with a wink. "Well, pick anywhere you'd like. I have a few other tables, but I'll be with you two in a minute."

I follow Jessie to a small booth in the back. She reaches for a sticky menu from the end of the table and reads it over and I follow suit.

Marsha returns quickly and takes our order. She's called away by someone in the back, so there's no further chitchat. In the wake of the silence, there's nothing left for us to do but talk about what we came here to talk about.

"So I was thinking about your situation," I start. "And I think you should try to get the community involved."

Her eyes narrow. "What do you mean?"

"Well, the village is only entertaining Mr. Tyson's offer because they need money, right?"

"Right."

"So they're not even thinking about what they might lose if they take his offer."

"You mean the Manor?" she asks.

"That, yes, but I was thinking some of the residents. If the village starts to lose its charm, how many of the lifelong residents will stick around? That's a more important tax base than some tourism dollars."

She grabs her straw between her lips and sips her water. "I think the village has already lost most of its charm."

"No, it's lost its businesses," I correct. "The bones are still here to go back to the way things were."

"What does that have to do with the community?"

"You just need to remind residents that there's still stuff here to be proud of. They'll start telling their friends who live elsewhere how great Montana Beach is and how much they like it here. Maybe they'll even start their own businesses here."

"And in the meantime, Mr. Tyson will buy up Montana Manor and leave me and my grandma homeless."

I shake my head. "No, because we'll start with the Manor."

"Huh?"

I can tell I'm rambling, so I take a second to collect my thoughts. "Okay, with all of the empty buildings down here, most of the community spends their days very isolated. Am I correct in that assumption?"

She shrugs. "I guess so. What makes you think that?"

"It's happening in small towns all across the country," I tell her. She gives me a skeptical look and I add, "I read a lot about this stuff."

"Right."

"Anyway, if they had a place to gather where they got to know their neighbors again and recreated a *community*, they would *care*, and therefore, be more likely to fight for what's still here."

"The Manor?"

"Yes." I flash a smile at her. "Among other places."

"So how do we do that?"

"By throwing a party at the Manor. Maybe a Fourth of July thing or something. Whatever will get people through the door, show them that you guys are still here and still just as classy as you've always been."

She grins.

"Make sure it's well-known that someone wants to tear it down and that you need their help."

"So we're throwing a party to save the Manor?"

"The party's where it starts. If you put together regular gatherings that remind people what they love about Montana Beach, they'll be more invested in keeping you here."

"Well, when I was younger there used to be a mid-summer parade that would end with a bonfire and beach party. We could bring back a version of that."

"Perfect!" I say with a smile. "That's exactly what we need. Something that'll ignite nostalgia in everyone and remind them what things used to be like while sparking hope for the future."

My phone starts buzzing beside me on the table. Dad. I hit ignore and turn it over.

"You're not going to answer that?" she asks.

"No, it's just junk," I tell her.

"All right, here we go," Marsha says with a tray resting on her shoulder. She sets each of our plates down and says, "If there's anything else you want, just let me know. Enjoy!"

I reach for the glass bottle of ketchup and slap the "57" until it plops all over my fries. "So what kind of budget do we have for this?"

Jessie pulls the pickles off her turkey sandwich. "What do you mean?"

"I mean, how much money do you have to spend on this? We'll need food, invitations, maybe some extra advertising. If it's for the Fourth of July, that's a little over a week away. We need to get going on this. It'll be small, but I think it'll be worth it."

"Yeah, I think we should get the word out as soon as possible." She picks up her sandwich and bites into it.

I pop a fry in my mouth. "So…the budget?"

"Oh, well, uh…"

"Jessie, it's okay," I say. "I'm not going to judge. I

just need to know so we can come up with a realistic plan."

"We don't have any," she admits. "We're just barely keeping our head above water as it is. If we want to keep feeding our residents and pay all our bills, we can't spend any more money on anything else."

"Oh wow." I thought she was just exaggerating before.

"Yeah."

"I knew you guys were struggling, but I didn't think it was *that* bad."

She shrugs and takes another bite. "Well, now you do."

I munch on a fry and stare at nothing in particular out the window as my mind turns. "Okay. We can still do this. Just let me think."

So no food at this party—or liquor. But the Manor *does* have the pool and it *is* beachside. But then, asking residents from a beach town to come to the beach isn't really a huge selling point. And there's no use trying to draw in people from North Beach. Their Fourth of July festivities will no doubt be miles ahead of anything little ol' Montana Beach can put together in a week's time.

"Your silence is scaring me," she says.

"Well, we're going to have to get creative, but we can do this."

"How?"

"Well, first off, scratch the invitations. We can't afford it."

"So how are we going to tell people about the party? Bulletin boards?"

I shake my head. "No. It's such a small community that we can probably go door-to-door inviting people. Actually, we'll probably be able to get more people to come if we make a personal connection. It's a lot better than an impersonal invitation."

"You think that'll work?" she asks skeptically.

"Sure it will. We can even bring a petition to save the Manor when we go around."

"Oh yeah, I didn't think of that."

"Does the village or anyone put on any sort of fireworks show for the Fourth?"

"Yeah, every year. Actually, the Manor usually has the best spot in town for it with all the balconies. But then, it's such a small town that I'm sure everyone can see them from their own front porch."

"But we need to tell people that Montana Manor is *the* place to watch them. Tell them to celebrate with friends and family or something. Maybe talk to Marsha here and see if she'd be willing to donate some burgers for an afternoon cookout."

Jessie looks hesitant. "Maybe."

"Do you want me to talk to her?"

She smiles. "I've never asked anyone for anything like that before. Not really, anyway."

"Well, sometimes you have to ask for help to get what you want."

"Isn't that the truth."

We throw around ideas as we finish our meal. Jessie wants to have a bonfire on the beach, but since it will be closed for the fireworks show, that's not going to work. I suggest we hold that off for the mid-summer party, but she seems nervous because I'll be gone when that party happens.

"You'll be fine." I snatch the check from the table and fish out some bills from my wallet.

"What do I owe?" she asks.

"I got it."

"Mason, come on. You're the one helping me out."

"It's okay. I had fun." I slip out of the booth and walk up to the counter before she can protest further.

There's a younger waitress working now. Brunette, probably in her early twenties. I wave the check and tell her, "I'm ready to pay."

"Oh sure," she says with a smile. She takes the receipt from me, punches it in the register and gives me the total. "I hope you enjoyed it," she adds.

"Oh, I did." I hand her the money. "But I was

wondering if I could talk to Marsha? I have kind of a weird question for her."

"Well, Marsha left for the day." The brunette—Ashley, according to her name tag—counts out the coins for my change. "Her shift ended at five. She's been here since we opened this morning."

"Ooo, that's rough. Well, I'll leave her alone then. I can come back later."

Ashley smiles. "I hope you do."

"Only so many places to eat in town." I take the change from her. "Bye!"

Back at the table, I leave a few bills and escort Jessie to the door. She turns right to head back to the Manor, but I grab her hand and motion in the opposite direction.

"What?"

"Let's take a walk."

She looks down the street toward the Manor and then back at me. "Mason, I really should get back."

"For what?" I ask. "The Newmans are having dinner elsewhere and the work's been done for the day. Besides, I haven't had the chance to properly explore this town. I'd love the tour from a local."

"Oh, you think you're so sly, don't you?" she says with a smirk.

"Just a walk, that's it." She doesn't look convinced,

so I add, "Come on, the sun's setting. We can go back once it's dark."

"Well, that sounds like the start of a horror movie."

I tilt my head down and look at her. "Please?"

She sighs, but still doesn't pull her hand from mine. "Okay. Sure."

We walk down First Street in the opposite direction of the Manor. She points out different buildings as we pass them.

"I had a friend in high school who's mom owned a bakery here. They lived above it in a tiny little apartment. Oh, and across the street over there was a used bookstore for a while. It was also a record store, and I think a pet store for a bit, too. Goldfish, mostly."

The street dead ends at Ocean Boulevard where the entrance to the pier begins with the small Ferris wheel at the end of it. Despite its size, it towers over the little town.

"That's where my best friend Robyn works." Jessie points down the pier. "Her and her family stayed with us a long time ago and we hit it off so well that we stayed in touch. When she graduated college, she moved down here and helped save this place when she became manager."

"Can we go check it out?"

Jessie shakes her head. "It's mostly just a kiddie

carnival now. The Ferris wheel is the only thing left that adults can go on. Actually, after the last storm I'm surprised it's still here."

"Does the beach get hit with a lot of hurricanes?"

"Not a ton, but it does happen," she says. "Usually it's just high winds, though."

We cross the street and start to head back in the direction of the Manor. She points to a building that looks abandoned at first glance. It's the first one on the street after the pier entrance. "The Nine" is etched into the glass window on the door that's off to the side.

"Downstairs is the bar another one of my friend's owns," she says.

"You've got a lot of friends here."

She shrugs. "It's a small town."

"What's the significance of the number nine?"

"It's a reference to the nine original residents of Montana Beach. It used to be a secret destination spot because of the way it's sandwiched between two wetlands, but it's grown a bit since then."

"I noticed there are only two roads in and out of town."

She nods. "It makes for less traffic noise, but it doesn't bring in any drive-by traffic, either. The only people who really come here are the people who already know about Montana Beach."

I laugh. "Not me. I just really needed to pee."

She swats at me and we keep walking until we reach Montana Boulevard. Ahead of us is the Manor, to the left is the beach.

"Wow, that sunset never gets old," I say, looking down the boulevard away from the beach. The last of the sun's rays stretch across the sleepy little town and makes everything feel so still.

"It's amazing."

"Should we go sit and enjoy it?" I nod to the small park just before the beach. There's a picnic table that's seen better days, but it holds when we take a seat.

She smiles. "It's moments like this that I love most about living here. The views, the solitude. I could deal with a few more people, but I'm glad that this is a small town. It's very relaxing."

I nod, still watching the way the sun hits the houses and trees throughout the town. "I agree."

A comfortable silence falls between us and I reach across the table for her hand again. She gives me a look, but doesn't pull away and quickly turns her attention back to the sunset.

The sun turns orange and the sky turns pink. This place is truly breathtaking. I've been here for a week and I'm just now realizing this. But when I turn to Jessie and see her leaning back with her eyes closed, soaking in the final rays of the day's sun, I know that nothing can beat the beauty of this woman sitting across from me.

Chapter Five:
JESSIE

I don't know what it is, but there's something almost invasive about walking up and knocking on a stranger's door. Even though I've lived in Montana Beach most of my life and I know basically everyone, it still doesn't feel right. Almost like I'm bothering them.

But, as Mason pointed out, I need to be able to ask for help in order to save the Manor. I'm just glad he's here with me. It was, after all, his suggestion that we approach people face-to-face.

"You ready?" Mason asks as we approach our first stop two doors down from the Manor. It's the first house on this street that isn't a vacant beach house rental.

"As ready as I'm going to be." I smooth out my yellow sundress with lilies on it. I thought it'd be a good idea to look nice. "Jump in if I start drowning."

He looks me over. "You look really nice. Beautiful, is actually the better word."

I tuck some of my hair behind my ear and look down to hide my smile. "Thanks."

He turns and rings the doorbell for me. Guess I already needed a nudge.

Mrs. Putney comes to the door in a T-shirt with seashells printed on it and white capri pants. She's a small older woman who moved here with her husband when I was a teenager.

"Good morning, Jessie," she says with a smile from the other side of the screen door.

"Morning!" I say cheerfully. Too cheerfully. That's not me. Ah, I need to stop trying so hard. "Do you have time to talk for a little bit?"

She looks up at Mason.

"Oh, this is my friend," I add. "This is Mason, he's one of our guests at the Manor."

Mrs. Putney opens the door and extends her hand to him. "Nice to meet you. Come on in, we can sit on the deck."

The Putney's house isn't massive, but it's nice. Every wall is painted white and the light hardwood floors extend from the entry in the living room all the way back to the kitchen, which leads to the covered deck overlooking the ocean.

"You have a beautiful house," Mason tells her as we take our seats outside. Mrs. Putney in a rocking chair, me and Mason on a swing hanging from the ceiling.

"Thank you. My husband and I fell in love with Montana Beach when we first decided to move down south. We just couldn't stand the cold weather in Chicago anymore." She looks over at us and gets to her feet. "Oh, where are my manners? Let me get you two some iced tea. Still learning this southern hospitality thing."

"No, it's okay." I motion to my bag sitting beneath the swing. "We're okay." I didn't know how long we'd be out here — all day, I'm assuming — so I brought water and some food.

"Are you sure?" She looks between us.

"Positive," Mason says with a charming smile. "Sit. Jessie has some stuff she wants to talk to you about. Is your husband around? We'd love to talk to him too."

Mrs. Putney points to a slouching man in a wide straw hat out on the beach. He trudges along waving his metal detector in front of him.

"He's out digging around. I love the man, but if I interrupt him now, I'll never hear the end of how he was *just* about to find something." She rolls her eyes with the hint of smile. "Been here almost fifteen years and still hasn't found anything worth more than ten bucks."

"Well, as long as he enjoys it," Mason says.

"It gets him walking around," Mrs. Putney says with a nod. "At least he's getting exercise."

"Well, we just wanted to drop by to talk to you about something concerning the whole town," I start, but Mason cuts me off.

"Do you live here all year? Or do you go up north for the holidays?"

Mrs. Putney watches her husband through the window. "No, we're here permanently now. We spend a week with our daughter for Christmas, but that's as much of the snow as we can take!"

We smile.

"And we have some friends who live more inland, so if the hurricanes ever come through, we'll have a place to go," she continues.

"It's good to have a backup plan," he says.

"Knock on wood that we don't have to fall back on that plan."

Both of them knock on the furniture they're sitting in and laugh.

"Like I was saying—"

"Do a lot of your friends or family ever come here to visit?" Mason says over me.

This is getting annoying. He told me that it'd be

better if I'm the one who talked more because I have the connection with these people.

"Once in a while our grandson will come and stay with us," she says. "We would love for him to be able to bring a few of his friends too, but we just don't have the room."

"Well, as I'm sure you know, Jessie and her grandmother run the Montana Manor, just a few doors down."

Ah, there it is. Nice segue, Mason.

Mrs. Putney offers a polite smile. "Yes, I'm aware. It's a very nice place to stay, but I doubt it's suitable for a group of college boys."

"Actually, I think it'd be the perfect place," I say. "My grandma's thrilled to have Mason staying with us."

Mrs. Putney holds her smile. "Yes, well, your friend here seems to be more polite than most young men."

"Even so, it's a good place to stay for people of all ages," I press on. "Close to the beach, near all the shops, easy to get to—"

"Jessie, sweetie, you don't have to sell me." Mrs. Putney holds up her hand to stop me. "Believe me, I know how wonderful your inn is."

"The trouble is, it might not be around much longer," Mason says.

"What?" She looks between the two of us, a hint of concern in her eyes. "What do you mean?"

"There's a man who wants to buy the Manor so he can tear it down for a resort hotel," I explain. "You know, one of those tall buildings that you see on the coast in North Beach?"

Mrs. Putney's concern turns to outrage. "Have you gone to the village about this? We like the small town! Sure, it'd be nice if the streets weren't so empty, but I don't want to see Montana Beach become so commercialized. There are already too many rental houses."

"I know," I say. "And I talked to the mayor directly. She said that because the village is desperate for money, they might have to push this deal through to get some. Otherwise, the village might be absorbed by North Beach."

"What does your grandmother say about this?"

I cringe. I haven't found the best way to tell her yet, but I know I need to. Soon. First, I'd like to have a good plan in place before I break the news.

"I thought it would be better to get the community involved to give her a better sense of hope before I told her," I say.

"How is the community supposed to help?"

Mason speaks up again. "Unless the residents of

Montana Beach voice their objection to this project—and put forth their best efforts to help draw people to the village—Montana Manor will be lost."

"Is there a petition? A rally? How can I help?"

"As a matter of fact…" I reach down and pull out a clipboard from my bag and hand it to her. "You'll be the first name on the list."

Mrs. Putney takes it from me and signs right away.

I take the clipboard back from her and stuff it in my bag. "We're throwing a Fourth of July party too. Montana Manor is one of the best places in town to watch the fireworks show. All you need to do is show up and have a good time. We're hoping the crowd will remind people how special the Manor—and the village—really are."

Mrs. Putney's face drops. "Oh, the fourth?"

"Is there a problem?" Mason asks.

"Well, my husband and I were thinking of going to North Beach for their…" She trails off, embarrassed. "You know what? Montana Beach is my home. We'll be there."

Beaming, I give her the details of the party and thank her for talking with us.

"I think that went well," Mason says once we're back on the sidewalk of First Street.

"Yeah, but if the rest of these visits take as long as

that, we'll be doing this for the next week."

"A week's worth of work to save your grandparents' lifelong dream?" Mason holds up both his hands, palms up like a scale. "Hmm, I think it's worth the sacrifice."

"Just don't cut me off next time."

"I was trying to establish a personal connection and have a conversation rather than make an impersonal pitch," he says. "These are your neighbors, not customers. Treat them like it."

He has a point.

The rest of the morning, we finish up visiting the houses on First Street, skip over most of Cemetery Street since a lot of them are rentals, and end up at the corner of Fifth Street and Montana Boulevard by time we decide to break for lunch.

Mason points across the street to the Savings Market, which takes up a whole block. "Want to see if we can get something in there? We probably should get out of the sun."

The village's only grocery store is an eyesore compared to the cute bungalows and beach houses on the neighboring streets. The way the heat waves reflect off the large open parking lot makes it one of the least desirable places to be on a hot sunny day.

"No, there's a park at the end of the street." I point

across Montana Boulevard. "Let's go there."

"What about food? I'm starving."

I pat my bag. "I've got it covered."

We find a spot under an oak tree in the park at the corner of Fifth Street and Ocean Boulevard behind St. Mary's Church. There's a playground, an overgrown baseball diamond, and painted lines for the community soccer field. Currently though, we're the only ones here. It's such a nice day that anyone who has time to be outside is probably near the water.

"Wow, this is nice," Mason says as he leans back against the tree with his hands behind his head. He closes his eyes and I watch for a second as the breeze blows in his short blond hair. I swear it's gotten lighter since he first came to the Manor. But then, he's probably just getting tanner.

Pulling myself back to reality, I pull out the lunch bag with deli sandwiches wrapped in plastic wrap. I nudge his arm and pass him his sandwich.

"Sorry it's warm. I couldn't find an ice pack in the freezer."

"Huh? Oh, thanks." He pulls it open. "I'm sure it'll be fine."

"We'll see." I reach for my own sandwich and unwrap it.

He takes a bite and chews for a bit. "You're always

so prepared. What are you, a Boy Scout?"

"Frugal is more like it." I pull out a Tupperware container of cantaloupe and dig around my bag for more. I groan when I come up empty. "Shoot. I thought I brought some cheese too, but I forgot it at home."

He laughs. "It's okay. This will be plenty."

"Are you sure? I could run to the store real quick or head back to the Manor—"

He grabs my hand and looks at me with humor in his eyes. "Jessie, it's fine. You need to learn to relax sometimes and just go with the flow."

"I can go with the flow!" I pull my hand away, annoyed at the jab.

He pops the lid off the Tupperware and picks a piece of cantaloupe with his bare hands. I pass him a plastic fork and he laughs. "What were you saying about going with the flow?"

"What? Just because I think we should use utensils to eat doesn't mean I'm uptight."

"Okay." He licks the juice off his fingers with a grin.

"Okay fine. I'm a little uptight," I admit. "I guess my five years in New York have stuck with me more than I thought." I take a bite of my sandwich and watch the wind blow in the trees.

His smiles fades. "New York? As in New York City?"

I look at him with a mouthful and mumble, "Yeah."

"When did you live there?"

I swallow. "The only time I didn't live here. I went to school up there for hotel management and got a job at one of the hotels in the city."

"And yet you still need my help to save your family's inn?"

I smack him lightly. "I just worked the front desk in New York, jerk! All I did was check people in."

"Where in the city did you live?"

"Astoria, but I worked in midtown." It's been a while since I've recalled my time in New York City to someone who actually knows about the places I'm talking about. "Hotel Richardson."

"Oh, okay! I used to work around the corner from there on Madison."

"Well, la di da, Mr. Hotshot."

He rolls his eyes. "Like you're one to talk."

I finish chewing my next bite and say, "And yet we both ended up here. How is that?"

"Life is funny that way, isn't it?" He pops the last of his sandwich in his mouth as I pick at the cantaloupe. Without a fork. I almost feel like I can't use one now that he's pointed it out.

I pack up our trash and hold out the container of fruit to him. "Want any more?"

He shakes his head, so I seal it up and stow it back in the lunch bag.

"What made you leave the city and come back here?" he asks.

I look down at my phone and say, "We have a bunch of other houses to hit. We should get going."

He grunts as he gets to his feet. When he raises his arms in the air, I get a glimpse of his belly. I've never really noticed before, but now I see how tan he is.

When he drops his arms down, he asks, "Where to, boss?"

The rest of the afternoon we visit the houses in the block bounded by Ocean Boulevard, Third, Atlantic, and Fifth Streets. When we finally arrive back at the Manor a little before six, Grandma is mad that she had to prepare dinner by herself.

"You could've at least *called*, sweetie," she tells me in the kitchen while Mason and the Newmans eat in the dining room. "It's the Newmans' last night, so I wanted to have a big send-off."

"Sorry, we lost track of time. But it looks like you managed everything here."

"You're lucky I've been doing this longer than you've been alive." Her glare softens and she reaches forward to move my hair out of my face. "So you had a good time with Mason today?"

I nod and try to remain expressionless, but the meaning behind Grandma's words makes me smile. "Yeah."

She pulls me in for a tight hug. "Oh, it's so nice to see you happy again."

"Grandma, it's not because of Mason," I say.

Pulling away, she gives me a goofy grin and says, "Sure, whatever you say, dear." She points to the dishes and adds, "Since you left me alone to cook, I'll leave you alone to clean. Unless you want to ask Mason for help?"

I roll my eyes and get started on scrubbing the dishes, doing my best to get the oven pan clean—looks like Grandma made turkey. I want to get the dishwasher loaded before everyone finishes dinner. If Mason came in here and offered to help, he'd stay and chat even if I told him I had it under control. Not that I'd mind him chatting, although I would get more looks from Grandma.

But Mason's on vacation. I can't let myself get too attached.

The next day follows the same pattern. This time, Mason and I cover the rest of Atlantic Street and the few houses on Sixth and Seventh Streets in the morning. I count up the names on the petition as we move from house-to-house. Up to almost two hundred now. That's nearly half the town!

Mr. Jameson in the small bungalow at the end of Atlantic Street is adamant about nothing changing in Montana Beach.

Nothing.

No new hotel, no new residents, no more traffic. Perhaps his attitude is a result of his tiny house being at the end of the street that leads right to the beach. His house is also sandwiched between two rental houses, so that could be a factor too. Or maybe he's just a grumpy old man. I don't think I've ever seen him smile.

The other neighbors—sporadically spread between several empty rental houses—seem supportive of keeping the Manor. All of them sign the petition and many of them agree to come to the Fourth of July party. By time Mason and I break for lunch at the park on Fifth Street, I have a good feeling about the fate of Montana Manor.

"I really think that we're on to something here." I dance as best as I can from my seat against the tree, shaking my shoulders and raising my hands in the air. "Thank you for helping me! This idea might just save the Manor!"

Mason grins as he kneels next to me, waiting for me to pull out the food from my bag. "Glad I could help.

It's a fun way to really get a feel for this town. It deserves some new life."

"You make it sound like it's dead." I pull out two yogurt cups. I wave the plastic spoon at him. "Don't be an animal, use this!"

"Yes, ma'am." He looks down at the ground with a smile.

"What?" I ask, still beaming from the success of our morning.

He licks his lips and looks like he's about to say something, but doesn't. Instead, he leans closer to me until his lips are pressed against mine.

I don't move, mixed with a feeling of surprise and a strong desire for it to last longer.

But he pulls away after a few seconds, the smile still spread across his face.

"I'm really glad I stumbled here," he says. "I couldn't think of a better place to spend the summer, or a better person to spend it with."

Suddenly realizing I'm still frozen in place, I try to play it off like the kiss didn't happen—like it didn't have such a profound effect on me. "Yeah, well, you're not too bad yourself. I've had worse summers."

He smiles again and I hope that means he knows that the kiss was special without me having to say it. I can only hope he feels the same way, except…

Summer Stay

What's going to happen when he goes back to New York City? When he returns to that fancy job on Madison Avenue? Surely, he won't remember the girl from the small beachside town he once kissed under a tree.

My rational self pulls us back to reality when I ask, "So what do you do? For a living, I mean."

"Why do you ask?"

"Most people aren't able to take four weeks off for a vacation. Even if they did, they wouldn't be this calm about not having a paycheck for a month."

He doesn't say anything, so I add, "What, are you rich or something?"

He chuckles. "No, I'm not rich. I just got a really big job offer and I don't know if I should take it. I'm probably just being stupid about it. It's a good offer and most people would be thrilled to have it, but it just doesn't feel right, you know?"

I nod.

"Besides, we should be concerned about you and saving *your* livelihood. So let's finish eating and hit the pavement."

Right. He doesn't want to talk about it.

I try to keep conversation to a minimum while we finish eating, but he coaxes words out of me with questions. All of which I'm happy to answer because nobody's really asked me them before. Not only that, but I can tell that Mason's genuinely interested in what I have to say. That he wants to know where I've come from and who I am right now.

He asks me about Robyn, Tyler, and Adrian — some of the friends I mentioned during our brief tour along First Street when he first agreed to help me save the Manor. He asks me more about my job in New York, if I still keep in touch with my friends from up there — I don't — and whether I'd ever consider going back — I won't.

A half hour goes by and I feel like all I've done is talk about myself. To my surprise, I'm no longer upset that Mason has been so private about the details of his life. I'm actually excited to uncover the secrets he holds so close. And I know just how foolish that is given my history with men. Well, one man in particular.

The next day, any worry I had about Mason and his feelings for me goes out the window. As much as I try to convince myself that it's better to distance myself from him, I can't help but want to spend all of my time with him. Not that that's hard with our mission to knock on every door in the village — there are a lot more than I thought.

By time we finally get the last resident to sign the petition, it's just after six-thirty. As we walk down

Montana Boulevard back down to the Manor, my stomach grumbles, my feet hurt, and my shoulders are on fire from the sun.

"I just want to thank you for spending the last few days with me," I tell him. "It really means a lot and I think it'll help make a difference. This party is going to be awesome."

He shakes his head and smiles, watching the sidewalk as we walk. "Not a problem."

I wish he would take my hand again, but his hands are buried deep in the pockets of his shorts. Clearly, he doesn't want to be close like that. I wonder if he's realized the same thing I have: this thing between us is temporary.

"I feel like I should pay you or something."

"Jessie, it's fine. You don't have to do anything."

"No, I do. What if I made you dinner?" I offer. "The Newmans are gone and you're our only guest. If I kick Grandma out, we could have the apartment to ourselves." Oh, that sounds bad. "To, um, talk and stuff—not *that* stuff, but…I don't know…you don't have to come, I guess. I was only offering since you've been such a big help."

He laughs. "That sounds nice. I'd like that. But I think I need a shower first."

Almost reflexively, I wipe the sweat from my brow.

"Right. I could use one too—by myself! I wasn't—that's not—I should stop talking now." Good thing my face is already red from the sun.

He laughs again. "That's not what I was thinking, but it's good to know where you stand on the subject."

The heat on my face from embarrassment is almost an inferno now. "How about this: we'll have dinner at say, eight o'clock? It'll give me time to shower and make dinner."

Mason nods. "Sounds like a plan."

I smile. "Good."

We're quiet the rest of the way—I'm nervous that I'll say something stupid again. When we get back to the Manor, we both head our separate ways: Mason to his room and me up to my apartment.

After a shower, I change into a nice shirt and jean shorts. I want to look good, but I also want to be able to play it off if he doesn't think of it as a date. *I* shouldn't even be thinking of it as a date. Of course, with the word vomit I had on our walk back, he probably thinks that I'm going to jump him as soon as he walks in the door.

Setting a pot of water on the stove to boil, I pull out a box of pasta from the cupboard as Grandma comes in from the balcony.

"Oh, there you are, sweetheart," she says. "I've been looking all over for you. I meant to call you earlier to see if you knew what Mason was doing for dinner."

"I'm actually making him dinner…for the two of us." I turn my back so I can't see Grandma's reaction. Still, I can hear the smile in her voice.

"Oooh." She draws out the word. "So I take it you want me to leave then?"

Glancing back at her, I say, "If you wouldn't mind."

She puts up her hands in surrender. "Consider me gone."

I turn back to the pot and stir the noodles. "There's something else I've been meaning to tell you."

"What's wrong?" Her voice is serious. She's always thinking the worst. Funny how things can change so quickly.

"I've been putting it off for a while, and I know this isn't the *best* time, but it's something you need to know."

"Well, spit it out!"

I turn to face her while I keep stirring. "There was a gentleman who came here about a week or so ago who was interested in buying the Manor from us."

"Oh." She looks thoughtfully at the messy counter for a few seconds and then adds, "In what context?"

"To demolish it."

"And you never told me about this?" Her voice raises.

"I wanted to have a plan to stop it before I told

you," I explain. "I shouldn't have kept it from you, though. I'm sorry."

"You're damn right you're sorry!" She sighs and says, "I hope you told him to buzz off."

"I did, but I talked to Patty Moore, the village mayor, and she said that even if we say no and he persists, the village might still be able to take the property away from us. No matter what we say."

Her shoulders slump and she plops in the wicker chair by the door. "So how long do we have?"

"It's not over yet, Gram. Mason's been helping me. It's where we've been going the last three days. We've been talking to the neighbors and we have a plan to stop Mr. Tyson's bid."

"All right, let's hear this plan."

"We're hosting a Fourth of July party!"

She's skeptical. "And *that's* going to save the Manor? Jessie, if you would've told me, we could've come up with a plan *together*! Mason's a nice boy, but he's our guest. He shouldn't be burdened with things like this. He's here to relax."

I nod, defeated.

"Now tell me how you think a party is going to save us."

"Well, the party's just part of it," I clarify, a little jilted that I didn't get the reaction from her that I expected. "Mason thinks that if the community is in support of us, the village will have to turn down Mr. Tyson's offer."

"Jessie, I'm just not sure it's that simple. Throwing a party—no matter how much everyone enjoys it—will not stop people with money, like this Mr. Tyson, from getting what they want. It's just the world we live in."

"Everyone's signed a petition too," I add with less enthusiasm.

She waves it off. "That doesn't necessarily change anything."

"At least it's a start. It's something!" I don't want to think about the fact that all the work Mason and I did these last few days has been for nothing. Not when it's built up so much hope for the Manor.

"You're right. It *is* something. I just don't think it'll be enough." She gets up from her seat and opens the door. "Let me know when you're all done up here so I can go to bed."

"Wait, where are you going?"

She sighs. "I need to think about things. I hope you two have fun, though."

Before I have a chance to say anything, the door closes and I'm left alone in the kitchen. I knew she wouldn't be happy about the possibility of losing the only real job she's had—not to mention our home—but I didn't think I'd feel this guilty for having kept it from her. I know her. That's what she was most upset about.

I turn off the stove, rinse the noodles in the strainer and mix them with sauce. After my talk with Grandma, I'm left with just enough time to set two plates before Mason comes.

The knock comes just at eight-oh-one.

I answer the door with a smile, but it immediately fades when I see that he's still in the same clothes as he was earlier today. He looks glum, but offers me a sad smile.

"Hey," he says.

I decide not to tell him that the food is literally on the table and try to block his view into the apartment. He looks nervous. Upset, even.

"You're right on time," I say with a forced smile. I know whatever he's about to say isn't good news.

"I'm really sorry, but I don't think I'm going to be able to stay for dinner," he says.

I try to remain nonchalant to the news, but my heart is in my stomach. "Oh okay. How come?"

He shakes his head and doesn't meet my eyes. "I just can't tonight. Maybe some other time. Before I leave."

I nod. Right, he's still leaving. Not that I didn't already know that. I was just hoping that maybe—of course he has to go back home. "Okay, sure."

"I'm really sorry."

"It's fine. Don't worry about it." He hesitates, so I add, "I'm actually pretty beat from being in the sun the last few days, so I might turn in early anyway. Good night!"

I close the door before he has a chance to say anything else. Now, not only do I feel guilty about keeping a huge secret from Grandma, but I feel incredibly lonely from being ditched. It hasn't turned out to be a good night.

Plopping down at the table behind one of the plates of spaghetti, I text my best friend Robyn.

It's been a crappy night already. I have food for two and no one to share it with. Want to come over?

I hit send and then quickly add, *Oh, and bring wine.*

Chapter Six:
MASON

"What can I get you?" the guy behind the bar asks. He looks a little younger than me. Darker hair and a gray T-shirt.

I scan the options on tap. "Uh…whatever you recommend. I'm not picky."

He grabs a clean glass from underneath the bar and fills it. When he sets it down in front of me, he says, "It's called Atlantic Ale. Brewed up in North Beach. On the sweeter side, but not too bad."

"Thanks."

"Enjoy." He steps over to get drinks for a group of people at the other end of the bar.

I pull a five out of my wallet and set it next to my drink. As I take my first sip, I look out through the window at the ocean. The sky is growing darker with each passing minute.

The Nine was the only place in town that seemed to serve alcohol. At least, it was the only place that looked clean. It doesn't feel like it's a basement bar, and yet it is. Once I got down here, I understood the appeal. The door behind the bar leads to a patio right on the beach. I'm kind of surprised it's here in Montana Beach. This place is like a hidden gem in a town on hard times.

As I watch the waves crash on the shore, I think about the turn of events this day took. I feel awful for ditching Jessie like I did. Especially because I could smell the food when she answered the door.

I just needed to take a break from everything after my latest phone conversation with my dad. If it could even be called a conversation. More like a berating. I wouldn't have been good company for Jessie and I don't want to rehash the whole story. Not tonight at least. Refusing to tell her would make her think I'm keeping something from her and that would do more damage than just blowing her off for one night.

I'll have to come up with an excuse for Jessie tomorrow. I don't want to think about all of my problems. I came here to forget them. Besides, at the moment with everything she could potentially lose, her problems are bigger than mine.

"So what's your deal, man?" the bartender says when he comes back.

"What do you mean?"

"You look like your dog just died." He laughs. "You're kind of killing the mood."

"Sorry, just going through a lot of stuff."

"Care to share?"

"Not really."

"Mind if I vent a bit, then?" he asks.

"Isn't it supposed to be the other way around? Aren't you supposed to be the wise one?"

"Ha! You're funny. Okay, fine, if you don't want to hear about my stuff, I won't tell you."

"Come on," I say in a defeated tone. "You can spill if you want."

"No, it's okay. I won't burden you." He offers his hand. "I'm Tyler, by the way."

"Mason. Nice to meet you." I know that name. "Are you friends with Jessie Ray? From Montana Manor?"

"Am I friends with Jessie?" He feigns exasperation. "Who *doesn't* know Jessie? Cute, blonde, kind of neurotic, but that's okay because we all love her." We both laugh. "Yeah, she's one of my best friends. I've known her since kindergarten, basically. You staying at the Manor, then?"

I nod. "Yeah, for two more weeks."

"So what brings you to this sleepy little town?"

"A long vacation."

"And I take it the vacation isn't as relaxing as you thought it'd be?" he asks.

"It's not that. I'm having a great time."

"Oh yeah, I can tell." He flashes a grin. "Sorry. Go on."

"I just got a phone call from home and it wasn't a good one. Completely ruined my day. I ditched my date—at least, I think it was a date." Better to leave Jessie's name out of it since Tyler knows her. "Maybe it was. I don't know. Either way, I'm hungry and miserable. I probably should've just kept my original plans."

"Well, I can't help you with your date or whatever's going on back home, but I can get you something to eat," he says. "On the house."

"You don't have to do that."

"Nonsense. The boss says to push the food to keep people here longer," he says with a smile. "Then they'll buy more drinks!"

"Well, if that's the case, I could use another one of these." I lift my empty glass up.

"Sure thing, man." He takes my glass, fills it, and then disappears around the corner to what I presume is the kitchen.

The crowd starts to roll in as I wait for my food. I recognize a lot of people from the last few days and now I regret coming here. But I'd feel bad about leaving with a complimentary meal on the way. That would be the second one I turned down today. And, of course, I still haven't finished my second drink yet. I can stick it out. Most of the older folks are heading out to the beachside patio, anyway.

The music volume jumps up when it hits nine o'clock. Nothing too bad, but I wasn't expecting this place to turn into a club. Definitely not what I had in mind for this evening. I'm about to get up to leave, but Tyler brings out my burger.

"Medium-well," he tells me, leaning in close so I can hear. "If you need anything, let me know."

"Thanks," I shout back, but I don't think my voice made it to his ears.

I chow down on my burger, noticing how the thumping music seems to have drawn in a younger crowd. They're probably staying in the rental houses Jessie and I skipped over this week. The small bar is full and it looks like the outside patio is too.

The Nine has a cool vibe. Exposed brick walls, wooden rafters, metallic ductwork. It's definitely obvious that it's been recently renovated. It's dark in here, but still classy. It reminds me of some of the bars back home.

No wonder I naturally gravitated to it. It's what I'm used to. Just like my current job with my father's company. It's comfortable. But just because something is comfortable doesn't mean it's the best thing for me.

A part of me wants to do something that scares me. Something exciting. Just like this trip. I didn't know where I was going. I just got in the car and went.

But I can't convince my father to see things from my side. Not when he's the one who moved our family into the city to begin with. He would take one look at this town and deem it a waste. In fact, he'd probably be trying to convince Jessie to take the deal from Mr. Tyson.

And he's very convincing. In the matter of a five minute phone call, he made me believe that I'm the dumbest person on the planet for even taking time to make a decision about his proposal. Told me that this "soul searching bullshit" has run its course and that I should return home immediately.

I'm pulled out of my head when I feel a gentle hand on my shoulder.

"Mind if I sit here?" Ashley from the diner asks.

I shake my head and motion to the seat beside me. She takes a seat.

"Where's your girlfriend?" She places her hand on my elbow and leans in to my ear.

"Jessie? She's not my girlfriend." Not after tonight, that's for sure. "I've been staying at Montana Manor for a few weeks now. She's just a friend."

That's not exactly true, I don't think, but it's the easiest answer. We haven't talked about any kind of romantic relationship, although I think it's obvious both of us are interested.

"Oh okay." Ashley straightens the cocktail napkin in front of her. "Where are you from?"

"New York City."

Her eyes grow wide with intrigue and then she leans close to me again to say, "I've never been there! How cool!"

"Yeah, it's definitely a whole different world." I glance up at the crowd walking in and catch sight of Jessie with another girl. I smile at her, hopeful that she'll forget I ditched her and we can salvage the evening now that I've had some space. She locks eyes with me and I notice the scowl that immediately crosses her face.

"I should probably go," I tell Ashley as I watch Jessie push through the crowd toward us.

She doesn't stop until she's right in front of me.

"Jessie, hi—"

Smack!

I get a slap right across my face.

It seems like the whole room is looking at me. It

might just be shock, but I swear the music stops for a second, too. I hold my burning cheek and look back toward the door as Jessie and her friend escape back up to the sidewalk.

"Are you okay?" Ashley asks from my side.

I nod before getting up to follow Jessie.

I break into a jog to catch up to her and call her name. Her friend gives me a warning look, but I grab ahold of Jessie's shoulder to stop her.

She spins around and shouts, "Stay away from me!"

"What's the matter?" I ask, but she turns to continue back to the Manor. "Jessie, I didn't do anything wrong!"

This stops her and she spins to face me again. "You know, I was really starting to like you, even though I knew I shouldn't. I thought you were different. I thought we had something going for us. But it turns out you're a liar just like the rest of them."

"Come on, let's just go back to your place," her friend says, pulling at her arm. Jessie ignores her.

"What are you talking about?" I ask. "If this is about ditching you for dinner, I'm sorry. I already apologized for that."

"How long have you been seeing her?"

I narrow my eyes. "What?"

"The waitress! Is she the reason you came here? Or did you just hit it off when you were at dinner with *me* the other night? You remember that? It was the night you held my hand and told me to show you around town." She rolls her eyes. "What a line."

"Come on, just forget it," her friend says.

"Jessie, believe me, we're not together," I say. "We were just talking about the city. I don't understand why you're going crazy when *nothing happened*!"

She wipes away the tears pooling from her eyes, her voice defeated. "Right. I'm the crazy one. Fantastic. Do you even know why I moved back home?"

"I don't know, your grandma's dying business?" Low blow. I regret that. Crap. "Jess, I didn't—"

"I found out my fiancé was cheating on me."

A silence falls between us. All I say is, "Oh."

"Yeah. So pardon me if seeing you with another girl is triggering for me."

"I'm sorry that happened to you, but that's not what's going on here," I say.

"Come on, Robyn, let's go," she tells her friend as she turns back to the Manor.

I pick up my pace and follow them. "Jessie, you're the reason I canceled our plans."

"Oh, that's great." She continues her power-walk without even a glance in my direction. "Decided you no longer liked me, huh? Or maybe it suddenly hit you that you've been leading me on."

"No, it's not like that. You're—you got in my head. You're confusing me. This decision I have to make is even more impossible than it was before."

"You're going to do what you want anyway," she says. "Just leave me alone until you go back home and we'll be good, okay? I'll get over it. I have before."

Realizing it's no use, I stop in my tracks with my shoulders slumped and watch her and Robyn until they reach the Manor. It's obvious she wants space. Probably hopes that I'll leave sooner than I am. At the moment, I half-consider it, but I'm not any closer to a decision about my future now than I was when I got here.

Jessie is absolutely the reason. When I came on this trip, I never intended to fall in love, which is exactly what happened. And now, she doesn't want to have anything to do with me.

Chapter Seven:
JESSIE

To my surprise—and disappointment—Mason listened to my request to leave me alone. It's been three days and neither of us have said anything to each other beyond the necessities.

Grandma noticed the change in our rapport immediately and hasn't been pushing us together as much. Nor has she really spoken about it. Maybe she remembers how devastated I was when I first moved back here.

Even though things between me and Mason have blown up, Grandma hasn't held a grudge or anything for keeping Mr. Tyson's offer from her. In fact, she's actually been helping me get everything ready for the Fourth of July party, which is *today*.

Summer Stay

With Mason keeping his distance, I had to get over my fear of asking for help and call Marsha at the First Street Diner to see if she would be willing to donate any kind of food for the party. Luckily, she agreed to send over some burgers and veggies to make salads.

Grandma's been cleaning the house with extra precision, which is saying a lot because she usually has such a high standard. She also insisted on buying what seems to be an endless supply of little American flags.

"It'll be fun to put them everywhere!" she told me when she brought them home. "We'll put them in every nook and cranny, so no matter where you look you'll feel patriotic."

Personally, I think it's a little much, but she seems excited about them, so I don't push it. And she hasn't mentioned her worry that this party isn't going to save the Manor, so that helps.

"It looks like it'll be a great day for a party," Mrs. Huber says at breakfast. She and her husband are a middle-aged couple who checked in last night for the holiday weekend.

"How many people are you expecting?" her husband asks us.

Instinctively, I look to Mason for help, but he keeps his eyes on his plate as he cuts into his French toast. "I really don't know, but the more the merrier," I say. "I think we'll have plenty of room regardless."

"I'm sure it'll be great," Mrs. Huber says.

When Grandma and I are cleaning up after breakfast, she runs off a list of things to do before everyone comes over.

"I'll finish up the dishes in here if you want to water the flowers." She maneuvers a pan in the sink so the water can rinse off the suds. "Don't forget the planters on the balconies or the ones in the front windows. Those have been getting droopy. Oh, and of course there's everything inside."

"I got it, Gram."

"After I finish up in here, I want to run the vacuum upstairs and make sure the open rooms are as tidied up as they can be."

"How many people are you expecting upstairs?"

"This party is supposed to remind people that we're here. We need to present our best self. Especially the rooms, where we want people to come and stay."

I nod. "Good point."

I leave her so I can start watering. There are a lot more plants than I thought. Usually Grandma handles it all, but she's going to be busy straightening up the rooms that probably look fine to me. And God knows she'll likely find something to be cleaned up or fixed.

I try putting off the planters on Mason's balcony,

but with all the other plants on the second floor watered, there's no other reason to put it off. Luckily, he shares it with the neighboring room, so hopefully I can get to it without seeing him.

But, of course, he's out on the balcony when I get out there. Sitting in an Adirondack chair with sunglasses and his shirt off, soaking up the sun. Like he needs to get any tanner.

"Oh. Hi," I say.

"Hi." He gets up and opens the door to his room. "I'll just get out of your way."

"Wait."

I let out a heavy breath. Avoiding each other like this is getting ridiculous. Time to call a truce. He doesn't have much time left here.

"I just wanted to apologize for my freak out the other day," I say. "I misunderstood what was going on and it brought back bad memories." Finally, I meet his eyes. "Sorry. You didn't deserve that."

He offers a tight smile. "Thanks. Now that I know what you've been through, I get it. It *did* look bad."

I tap my nails on the side of the watering can. "Yeah."

There's an awkward silence that fills the space between us, but he finally breaks it when he says, "Well, you probably have a bunch to do before the party. Let me know if you need anything."

"Actually, there is something. We need someone to man the grill later. I asked my friend Adrian, but he has to work. Would you be up for it?" I flash him a smile, which comes easy. "Just don't give anyone food poisoning."

He laughs. "I'll try not to."

"Thanks." I look out at the ocean to avoid looking at him. I should go, but something keeps me here.

"No problem."

"Well, I should get back to work, then." I escape through the closest door, which happens to lead into Mason's room. My cheeks burn once I realize it, but I push myself to ignore it and find the rest of the plants in the house. There's too much to do to worry about embarrassment.

Grandma and I run around like crazy people until the grandfather clock in the living room dings, signifying one o'clock. We both head back up to our apartment and get ready for the party. I put on a white sundress and Grandma dons a red shirt with an American flag bedazzled on it and white pants.

"Well, don't you look spiffy, dear," she says as we head back downstairs.

I give a little curtsy. "You too, madam."

In the kitchen, I pull a veggie tray out of the fridge

and set it on the dining room table. Grandma sets out bowls of chips and I fill a pitcher with water and another with sweet tea.

Mason comes down in a white button-down and shorts. "Should I start the burgers?"

"Not now," Grandma says. "It's still early. Let's see what everyone wants first."

"Sounds good," he says. "We told everyone two, right?"

I glance over and see it's just about two o'clock. "Yup. They should be here anytime now."

"Well, everything's all set," Grandma says. "There's nothing left to do but wait. I'll leave the door open so everyone can come in when they get here."

We move out to the patio near the pool where the Hubers join us within a few minutes. The five of us chit chat about the weather, the fireworks show, and some of the food, but the conversation quickly dies off.

I pull up my phone and scroll through Facebook. My event about the party doesn't have a lot of people listed as "Going." Only five, actually. One of them being me. There are about fifty people who said "Interested," but I wonder if they'll even remember.

The fact that Mason and I went door-to-door inviting people and yet nobody's here sucks. I feel discouraged and definitely grim about the future of the

Manor. A lot of people said they'd come and not one of them could show up?

After an hour and a half of waiting, Grandma says with a heavy sigh, "Well, I should probably go put the veggies back in the fridge. I'm not sure anyone's coming."

The disappointed look in her eyes nearly crushes me. I quickly excuse myself and head out around the fence to the beach where nobody can see me. Out in the sand, there are several groups of people who are clearly out celebrating the holiday weekend. The bitter part of me wonders why they can't stop by our party. Don't they care? Won't they miss us once we're gone?

"Jessie, wait," Mason calls from behind me.

I let him catch up and wipe at my eyes. This is the second time he's seen me cry.

"It's still early," he says. "Maybe people will come later."

I scoff. "I doubt it. Nobody cares about the Manor anymore. They can't even be bothered to come to a free party. Message received, this town is dead in the water and we're next in line to go."

"Don't say that." He pulls me into a hug.

"I just wish Grandma didn't have to watch all of this slip through her hands," I mutter into his chest. "This is her whole life and now it's being ripped away from her."

"Hey." He holds me out at arms-length. "It's not

over. You're going to learn from this, and the next party will be even better and you'll get more people to support you guys."

"You won't be here to help." I avoid his eyes and look out at the water. It's my escape from everything. I wonder if it's what drew Mason here in the first place.

"You don't need me."

I don't say anything.

He slips his hands in his pockets and looks up at the Manor. "I've only got another week here."

"I know."

"I'm going to miss it."

"Yeah?"

He nods. "And you."

This gets my full attention. I let myself admit, "I'll miss you, too."

Mason looks down as he kicks at the sand with his bare feet. "I, uh, haven't been completely honest with you."

My heart beats a little faster. I don't know why I'm worried what he's going to say. I already went through this panic mode earlier this week. I've already damned him as much as I can in my mind. What's another reason to write him off?

But the first reason was bogus. And there is *absolutely* reason to panic about what he's going to say because other than the fact that he lives almost seven hundred miles away, he's perfect. Or damn near close to it.

"When I first came here, I was trying to escape from my life in New York," he says. "My dad is the CEO of a big advertising agency and he offered to train me so I can take over for him. It scared me—still does—but it'd be a good job."

"Sounds like your mind's made up then." The wind blows my hair in my face and I tuck it behind my ear to move it away.

"But it's not." He takes my hands. "Jessie, when I was driving down here, I didn't know where I was going. I just knew I needed to get away. Find someplace where I could relax and clear my head so I could go back home with a fresh start. I thought it was inevitable that I would replace my father at his company and that this trip was my last chance at relaxation."

"And then you met me and I filled your time with things to do instead of leave you alone to enjoy your trip."

He squeezes my hands. "No. I met you and you made me question everything I thought I knew. Jessie, I'm completely taken by you. More than I've ever been with any other girl. You're beautiful and smart and hardworking and you care a lot about your grandma and continuing her dream."

I'm embarrassed to be grinning like a goof, so I turn my head to watch the waves again. Another escape. What he's saying is all very nice to hear, but it still doesn't change the fact that he lives so far away. This relationship, or whatever it is, isn't going anywhere.

"Now that my time in Montana Beach is ending," he continues, "I'm even more confused about what I should do. I never expected to fall in love with someone, but I did."

My eyes snap back to his. "What?"

He smiles. "I love you, Jessie."

All the air seems to be sucked out of me. How can he be sure he loves me? We've only known each other three weeks! Up until a few minutes ago, I didn't even know what he did for a living. This morning we still weren't speaking. This is just a vacation fling that got carried away.

"Wow." I chew on my bottom lip as I consider what else I'm going to tell him. "Uh…thank you."

He tries to mask his disappointment with a smile, but I can still see it, which eats at me.

"Mason, it's not that I—"

"Jessie!" Grandma calls from the patio. "There's a Jack Tyson here who wants to speak with you."

Oh crap.

Letting go of Mason's hands, I race back to the Manor. This is not a good time for him to show up. Not in the middle of our pitiful party. But then, maybe we can play it off like we're just hanging out. Maybe we don't have to tell him that we had intended for there to be a party.

He's in a baby blue button-down shirt tucked into his khaki shorts and his feet are covered in brown loafers without any socks.

"Miss Ray, nice to see you again," he says when I step onto the deck.

Grandma and the Hubers are still here and Mason is right behind me.

"Shall we go inside and talk?" Mr. Tyson asks.

I shake my head. "No. We can talk out here."

He looks over at the Hubers and then back to me. "Very well. I heard from some of the neighbors that you're throwing a party. How charming. Is it over already?"

I cross my arms. "If you think this is going to make us reconsider selling, then—"

"You're right. I'm sorry. I didn't mean to insult you," he says. "I was visiting a friend who lives in town with a perfect view of the beach and I thought I'd drop by to see if you and I could work out a quick deal. If not,

I plan on getting in touch with the village officials on Monday."

Noting the nervous look on my grandmother's face, I tell Mr. Tyson, "We haven't changed our minds. This is our home and this is our heritage. We're not going to give it up easily."

"Miss Ray, I urge you to reconsider," he pushes. "If this goes through eminent domain, you likely won't get top dollar. Only what the property is assessed for. If you sell to me directly—"

"I believe my granddaughter already gave you our answer," Grandma says, coming up behind me and resting her hands on my shoulders. "Now, if you're here to enjoy the party, please, pull up a chair. But I will no longer entertain the idea of selling our property to anyone."

Mr. Tyson looks between us with a conceited grin. "Okay. Well, sorry to bother you, ladies. I should head back anyway. Enjoy your party."

I wait until I see him slip out the front door before I turn and hug Grandma. "That was awesome!"

She pats my back. "Yes, well, hopefully the village doesn't give in to his demands. Something about that man..." She shivers.

"Well," Mr. Huber says, "I say pop a cold one and savor his absence for the time being. This is a party, after all!"

"Yeah!" his wife says. "No matter how small!"

It's moments like these that make me really love my job. Being able to meet sweet people like the Hubers. And Mason. He's been a big help in trying to save the Manor, even if it might not be enough.

But for the rest of today, I'm not going to worry about it. Taking Mr. Huber's advice, I grab a drink from the fridge, pull up a chair on the patio, and enjoy the moment.

When I worked in New York, I never got to personally know the guests I worked with. Not like at Montana Manor. I met Robyn here, I met Mason here, and now, I'm getting to know the Hubers.

They tell me about their daughter who is about my age and is a travel writer for Conde Nast. Mrs. Huber shows me pictures her daughter has sent them from Paris, Thailand, Argentina, Alaska, among so many others.

They tell me about their home outside of Pittsburgh, about their careers as teachers, how they want to start traveling in their retirement. In return, Grandma and I share stories about growing up at the Manor and the few strange guests we've had.

When the sun is just starting to turn orange, I hear voices from in the house.

"Hello? Are we too late for the party?" It's the Putneys.

Grandma jumps up and greets them. "Oh, you made it!"

I glance at my phone. Just before seven. Five hours late is better than not showing at all, I guess.

"Sorry we're so late." Mrs. Putney hooks a thumb to her husband. "*Someone* insisted on going out and getting some *exercise*."

"I found a dime from 1904 today!" Mr. Putney exclaims as justification for his outing.

I take a large cake pan from him and set it on the dining room table.

"I made my mother's German chocolate cake," Mrs. Putney tells us. "I didn't want to come empty handed."

"Oh, you didn't have to go through the trouble," Grandma says. "But it looks delicious. Thank you!"

"Not a problem, dear."

By time Grandma and I have pulled out the veggie tray and the beverages, another couple peek their heads in the door. "Hello?"

"Dolores!" Grandma shouts and runs up to the newcomer to hug her. "You made it!"

"Wouldn't miss it, honey," she says. "You remember Bill?"

"Of course!"

I escape out onto the deck to tell Mason to fire up

the grill. The sun is just starting to set, but more and more guests trickle in until there are people packed on the back patio and scattered in the living room and dining room. Just as I'd hoped, our party provides the perfect excuse to bring the neighbors together again to catch up.

I weave through the crowd, offering drinks, pointing out the pool, bathrooms, and even talk to one older man about our rates. Finally, after a couple hours pass and the sun is just about gone, everyone has seemed to have found a seat and eating the burgers Mason cooked up.

"Looks like everything turned out after all," Mason tells me when I'm next in line for my burger.

"Yes." I lean up and kiss his cheek. "Thank you so much."

"Hey, you did most of the work. I just gave you a nudge."

"Well, I appreciate it. I guess I needed the push."

"You're welcome."

"Looks like they're starting to set up for the fireworks," Mrs. Huber calls out, breaking into mine and Mason's moment.

"They're going to close the beach while they set them off." Grandma stands in the doorway and shouts to everyone both outside and in. "If you can't find a comfortable spot out here, we have plenty of balcony space upstairs."

Everyone settles into a spot throughout the house. Mason and I sit on the edge of the patio that leads to the beach so we can stop anyone from leaving the deck during the fireworks show.

He wraps his arms around me and kisses my cheek. Even if it is just a summer fling—which I very much wanted to avoid—I decide to let it be and enjoy the moment. It might not last forever, but right here and right now, this is perfect.

Looking around at the number of people who came to support us, I get the feeling that my smile will be permanently planted on my face. Even if we lose the Manor, I know everything will work out. If nothing else, Grandma and I will have moments like these to remember for the rest of our lives.

Chapter Eight:
MASON

"Yeah, Dad, I'll be home late Friday," I say into the phone as I set a folded pair of shorts in my suitcase.

"So should I write up a press release announcing your intent to take over for me?" he asks on the other end.

"We'll talk when I get back." I don't want to make any promises because I'm still not sure myself. Choosing to work for my father's company is the most logical choice and smartest move, financially speaking, but I'm not convinced it's the right move.

"I would think that a month off to 'find yourself,' or whatever it is you're doing, would be enough to help you see reality."

"I'll text you when I'm heading out." Avoid

confrontation. That's the best way to handle my father's jabs. He acts as if I'm his only kid who needs a vacation. "Tell Mom I miss her and I'll see her soon."

"Okay, son. See you later this week. Be safe driving back."

"Bye Dad."

I toss my phone on my bed and take a look at the clean clothes resting in my suitcase. It seems like I was just *unpacking* everything. I still have a few days, but I thought I'd get a jump on packing so I don't have to worry about it later.

It's bittersweet to know I'm leaving. I miss my family and friends back home, but I know I'll miss Jessie and Ethel and the Manor, and this town, too. Maybe I'll just miss being able to do whatever I want here, but I didn't mind the days I spent with Jessie going around town "working." It was actually fun.

The clock on the bedside table shows that it's just after nine, so I head down to breakfast. My plate is the only one still on the table. There's a lid over it to keep it warm. I wonder how long it's been there.

"If that's gone cold, dear, we can heat it up for you," Ethel tells me as she bustles around the house with a watering can.

"I'm sure it's fine," I tell her. "Thank you, though. It looks delicious."

I take a seat and start to dig in. Sausage, hash browns, and toast. Simple, but just enough.

Jessie comes through the kitchen door drying her hands in a dish towel. She's wearing a blue T-shirt and shorts and her hair is up with a clip. She looks stunning.

"Oh, I wasn't sure if you were coming," she says. "How's it taste?"

"Good." I indicate the chair across from me. "Do you have time to join me?"

Looking around to see her grandmother's disappeared upstairs, she pulls out a chair and sits down.

"So…you've only got a few more days left," she says.

I shovel some of the hash browns onto my fork. "Yeah."

"Have you decided what you're going to do?"

We haven't really talked about my job since the Fourth of July party last weekend. Haven't really talked about us or the fact that I told her I love her. It's obvious everything's on both of our minds, though. Somehow, without really making plans ahead of time, we've managed to spend every day with each other since then.

I've been joining her on her morning runs more frequently. She's been taking longer breaks with me by the pool. We always somehow end up in the kitchen together at lunch time. And in the evenings, after dinner's been cleared, we've been taking walks through town, talking until the sun has completely set.

This is what two people in love do. They're drawn together by a force much greater than either of them can comprehend. Only, I'm the only one who's said it out loud. Each passing day it becomes more obvious that she feels the same way, yet she refuses to admit it. That tells me that my summer vacation really is coming to an end.

"I'm going back to New York City." I keep my eyes on my plate. "I'll take up my dad on his offer."

I glance up in time to see her nod just before I drop my gaze back down.

"I guess that makes sense," she says. I might be reading into it, but it sounds like the life has been ripped from her voice.

"Yeah."

It's probably for the best. What would I do for a job if I stayed here? There's no advertising agencies around. Not even any businesses that could afford a marketing person. I'd probably have to commute to North Beach or somewhere further for work. Or worse, work at the gas station or grocery store in town. Even though I'd be with Jessie, I know I wouldn't truly be happy with that life.

Besides, if I lived and worked in paradise, would it continue to feel like paradise? Especially if I moved here for a woman who can't even tell me she loves me.

"Well, I've got a bunch of work to do," she says, pulling me out of my thoughts.

"Any new guests?" Now that the Hubers have checked out, I'm the only one here. I don't like the idea that this place will be without a guest, even for a little while.

"Yeah, we actually have two new couples coming in tomorrow and the next day."

"So the party helped?"

She shrugs. "I guess, yeah. I'm not sure it'll save this place, but at least it reminded people that we're here. Actually, the one couple is coming to visit the Clintons. You remember them? They were at the party."

I rest my head on my hand and squeeze my eyes shut as I think. "Oh, they live on Fourth, right? Across from the school?"

She nods. "Yup, big blue house. Apparently, they're in the middle of renovations and don't really have a room set up to host guests."

"That's good. Hopefully you can get more people like that."

"Yeah," she says with a sigh.

"What's the matter?"

"Well, you and I both know that a few extra guests here and there isn't going to save this place. This time next year the Clintons will be done with their renovations and when their friends come visit, they'll just stay with them. We're targeting the wrong people."

"Maybe," I admit. "But it's a start."

"The start of a battle I'm not sure I'm equipped to fight. At least not alone."

"What do you mean?"

"I'm not like you. I only know how to run the day-to-day operations of a hotel. I'm not good at advertising or marketing ourselves. I need someone like you to worry about that stuff."

I don't say anything at first. It's the closest she's come to saying she wants me to stay. But why can't she come out and say it? And how would it even work? If I moved down here, they couldn't afford to pay me. It's just better if I go back home. Jessie and Ethel can manage this place on their own. They always have.

"So we're kind of back at square one," she says.

"You don't want to put together another party?"

"I don't really see the point."

"I thought you wanted to revive the midsummer party?"

"To bring in more friends of locals who will eventually just stay with their friends?"

"Well, that's a pessimistic attitude."

"I'd call it a realistic one," she says.

"Whatever. *I* think the Fourth of July party was a

success," I say. "Slow to start, that's for sure, but a good sign for the future."

"I can't say I agree."

I finish up what's on my plate, set my fork down and look across the table at her. "What's really bothering you?"

"Nothing's bothering me." She takes my plate and carries it to the kitchen.

I get up and follow her. "Well, that's a lie."

"Mason, just let it go. I don't want to have the party, okay?" She rinses the plate off in the sink and sets it in the dishwasher.

"So you're not even going to try to save your home? What happened to all that stuff about this being your grandparents' dream and your livelihood? Was that just crap to get Mr. Tyson out of your hair?"

"No, it wasn't—"

"Then what was it?"

She slams the dishwasher door closed. "What does it matter to you anyway? You're leaving. By this time next week, you'll be back in New York and probably forget all about us."

I bite my bottom lip to keep from saying anything else.

"Grandma and I will be okay, no matter how this turns out," she adds.

"What about your friends?"

"What about them?"

"Didn't you say you know the owner of the Nine? I met your friend Tyler there the other day. And you said Robyn works at the Pier, right?"

From the corners of her mouth I can see a hint of a smile because I remembered some details of her life.

"What does that have to do with the Manor?" she asks.

"You could host a fundraiser at the Nine. If it's there, you're more likely to get walk-ins. And you can serve alcohol, plus you could negotiate with your friend to get a nice chunk of the profits."

She nods. "Not a bad idea, I guess."

"You could have door prizes or a basket raffle or something. Give away a gift certificate to the First Street Diner, the Pier, and other local businesses. Draw people in and keep them here by reminding them that this town still has stuff to offer."

"But who's going to help me plan it?" she asks. "You're leaving at the end of the week."

I look down and nod slowly. "Yeah, I am."

"You've got all the good ideas on how to run these sorts of things."

"Jessie, I'm sure that you guys can pull it off. Ask your friends for help. Even if the party's not perfect, it's still better than not throwing one at all."

"Yeah, but…"

"But what?" I take a step toward her.

Jessie looks up at me. "You won't be there."

I give her a sad smile and wrap my arms around her. Since the party, we've only kissed a handful of times. Most of the time it was a good night kiss when *she* walked me to *my* door because she didn't want her grandmother to see. Now, I'm not sure if I should try to kiss her. But man, I want to.

"We still have all week," I tell her. "Let's spend it together, like we've been. We can hang out at the beach, go for walks, do whatever you want to do."

She pulls away. "I don't know. There's a lot to get done around here and for the party. Grandma can't do it all herself."

"Okay, then I can help you finish the chores around here so we can —"

"No, Mason. We can't keep kidding ourselves. By this time next week, we'll be over. I didn't even want it to start in the first place."

Well, that's a punch in the gut. "Oh. Okay."

She looks at me and takes a deep breath. "I didn't mean it like that. It's been fun, but I just think that we shouldn't get too caught up."

I nod and try not to think about how I made it

obvious that I *am* 'caught up.' "Right, makes sense. I'll just, uh, be upstairs getting some of my things together. You do what you gotta do. If we meet up later, that's cool. If not…cool."

When I turn to head back up the stairs like a dog with its tail between its legs, I can almost feel her sorrowful eyes on me.

I get it. She doesn't want to continue to get close to me if I'm just going to leave. Especially after what happened with her and her fiancé. I think she knows by now that I'm not like him, which is why she let herself indulge this much.

But doesn't she realize that if she just admitted how she felt and asked me to stay that I would consider it? Of course, I probably could also come right out and *tell* her that's what I want.

So why haven't I? Is it because she's already basically rejected me once by not telling me she loves me when I *know* she does? Or is it the uncertainty of what life would be like if I decided to make Montana Beach my home?

I love Jessie, but we've only known each other just about a month. What if it doesn't work out? What happens when the fairytale of the summer ends? What happens if I make the wrong decision and regret it?

The sun has already given me a very nice tan for the summer, but I figure a few more days of the rays are necessary to really soak up what's left of my trip. Besides, after Jessie basically shut me out this morning, I figure I have nothing else to do.

After an hour out on the beach trying to ride some waves in the ocean, I quickly grow bored and come back to the Manor, sandy and soaking wet from a mixture of sweat and ocean water.

"It's nice out there, isn't it?" Ethel's wiping off the lounge chairs in the pool area with a rag.

"Yeah, but also kind of weird to be the only one on the beach on such a gorgeous day."

"Wait until later in the afternoon when the sun cools down a bit. Then more people will be out there."

"Well, I also came in because I was getting hungry." I turn the knob for the outdoor shower and rinse my feet off.

Ethel comes closer and drops her voice. "Now, I know it's none of my business, but I just thought you should know something before you go. I think my Jessie Girl is crazy about you. I haven't seen her this happy since she announced she was getting married back when she lived up in crazy town — I mean, New York City."

I smile.

"Has she told you about him?"

I nod.

"That man hurt her more than she lets on and I think she's still a little fearful that someone else will hurt her like that. So don't hold it against her that she can't come out and tell you how she feels just yet. Give her time."

I nod. "I'll keep that in mind, thanks."

She holds up a finger and adds, "And if you hurt her in any way, I'll show what real crazy is like." She snaps my butt with the rag and turns to go back in the house.

With Ethel's words still ringing in my ears, I decide to hang out by the pool the rest of the day in case there's an opportunity to talk to Jessie.

All day, I catch her stealing glances from various places in the house. In the window by the stairs while she's dusting. Off one of the balconies upstairs when she's watering. Through the doors leading to the dining room as the sun disappears on the other side of the house.

I stay out by the pool until the sun has officially set, hoping that Jessie will come out and at least sit by me like she's been all week before our conversation this morning. But she doesn't.

As I trudge up the stairs to shower before dinner, I can't help but feel disappointed. I really thought she'd say something or do something to indicate that she wants me to stay. Guess I don't know her as well as I thought.

The shower reminds me just how long I've been in the sun. Even with the water as cold as I can get it, the spray from the shower head still feels too hot on my shoulders. I'll have to stay out of the sun the next few days so I'm not itching all the way home.

When I get out of the shower, I wrap a towel around my waist and grab the aloe vera from my bag. As I rub some onto my shoulders, there's a knock on the door. I see Jessie through the peephole.

"Hey," I say when I open it. "Come in."

She looks down at my towel and then back up to my eyes. "Oh, sorry. Should I come back?"

"No, it's fine." I hold out the bottle of aloe. "Actually, could you do me a favor?"

She looks at me nervously. "You want me to put that on you?"

I hand her the bottle. "If you don't mind."

"Oh. Yeah. No problem."

"Thanks." I take a seat on the edge of the bed and feel it shift as she climbs up behind me. "Guess I was outside too long today."

"How's this feel?" I feel the cool lotion on my skin

as she rubs it in. Immediate relief washes over me.

"Really good. Thanks. I'm sure this isn't what you came up here for, though."

"I just wanted to talk to you about what we discussed this morning," she starts. "Mason, this is really hot—I mean, *you're* really hot—I mean, you're burnt."

I laugh. "Oh yeah? Well, you're not so bad yourself."

"Anyway…" She rubs more onto my shoulders. "I just wanted to say that I'm sorry for sending you mixed signals. I got carried away the last few days and I guess I just tried to ignore the fact that we come from two different worlds."

"No, we don't."

"We live almost seven hundred miles apart."

"And yet we ended up here together." I turn and take the bottle from her. "Jessie, I'm not afraid to tell you that I love you. Because I do. And it's not something that'll end when the weather cools down. I love everything I know about you so far and I can't wait to learn more. So what if I live far away? We can make it work. Maybe—"

Her lips on mine cut me off mid-sentence. It takes me by surprise at first, but then I feel her arms wrap around me and I pull her onto my lap. She pushes me back flat on the bed and we kiss for a bit before I break it off.

"What's this?" I ask, sitting up on my elbows.

"I don't know where this will go or where we'll end up," she says, her chest still heaving with heavy breaths. "All I know is that I don't want to think about the future anymore today. I just want you to hold me and make everything okay." She leans down and kisses me once. "Can you do that?"

Pulling her down, I bring my mouth to hers and we both give in to the passion we have for each other. Even though she still hasn't said she loves me, her actions show that she does. She'll tell me soon enough.

Chapter Nine:
JESSIE

"Mmm, where are you going?" Mason grumbles beside me as I swing my legs onto the floor.

"I have my chores to do." I lean down and kiss him on the cheek. "Don't worry, I'm not running out."

He wraps his arms around my waist and pulls me back onto the bed. "Can't you sleep in just one day? I'm the only one with a room booked."

I pat his arms locked around me. "Even so, we have some folks checking in today and I still need to get their room in order and all the office stuff. You can help if you want."

Prying apart his arms, I stand and reach to the ceiling as I stretch.

Mason sits up and rubs his eyes. "Okay, fine, I'll help. I take it you're still going to want to go for your usual run?"

"Yup!" I say cheerfully. On purpose, of course, to annoy him with how quickly I wake up even before the sun. "Come on, you're making me late."

"I'm coming. Give me ten minutes to change and I'll meet you down on the beach."

I lean over the bed one last time to kiss him before heading up to my apartment to change.

I've only spent the night in one of the rooms once and that was when Robyn was staying with us during one of her college breaks. And even that was by accident. We had too much to drink and I passed out on the armchair. Not that exciting, but definitely enough to remember.

Grandma's bedroom door is closed and I don't see any sign of light coming from the cracks when I sneak up to my room. She must still be in bed. Won't be long now, though.

Back down on the beach, Mason is sitting in the sand, stretching forward to touch his toes.

"You know, I've done this with you for the better part of four weeks and I *still* don't understand how you can do this so early in the morning," he says with a yawn.

I take a seat next to him and tuck my feet together

to do butterfly stretches. "Well, as you've pointed out, you've been running almost every morning, which means you've been able to do it too."

"Doesn't mean I like it."

"It grows on you." I turn in a new position to stretch.

"I bet a lot of things just have to grow on you, huh?"

I shoot him a look and hop back up to my feet. "Let's go. The sun is cresting."

On the count of three, we take off. I let him keep up with me, even let him pass me a little bit, but by time we hit the halfway mark and start back to the Manor, I pick up my pace and leave him in the dust. I don't slow until I've made it back to the patio off the Manor, sweaty and breathless, but otherwise refreshed.

Within a minute he joins me, panting and sweating. "You hustled me, Jess."

I laugh. "I do it every morning, you should know by now what I'm capable of."

"You're full of surprises, that's for sure." Pressing me against the wall beside the door, he kisses me like he did last night, pressing his body against mine in the morning sunrise.

Last night was the tipping point in my reluctance to be with him.

D. Allen

Clearly.

I keep reminding myself that even though he's only here for a few more days, it's better to make the most of it. Otherwise, I'd only be left to wonder what would've happened. I'll just try not to think about him leaving at the end of the week.

Yeah, like that'll work.

Grandma catches me when I get back to our apartment to shower. She's standing behind the kitchen island pouring herself some coffee.

"Did you have a nice run, dear?"

"Yup." Best to keep responses to a minimum. This woman somehow knows everything.

"Hope you didn't wake Mason." She stirs sugar into her cup and offers me a smirk.

"Uh…he said he wanted to come with me, so he's up already." I point to the bathroom. "Do you need to get there?"

She shakes her head, the smile still present.

By the time I get out, Grandma's moved to our balcony, seated in an old wicker chair with most of the white paint worn off.

"All cooled down, then?" she asks.

"Uh, yeah. Ready for the day. Don't worry about breakfast. I can get it. It's just Mason."

"Oh no, I can't let you do it all by yourself." She sits

up. "He's our only guest and it's his last week. We should make him feel as comfortable as the day he arrived!"

"I will!" My voice jumps. I'm too preoccupied thinking about the way he kissed me downstairs. "I just don't think there needs to be two cooks in the kitchen for one guest."

She leans back. "Very well, then. You two have fun. I hope you've been keeping him company."

I rub at my neck. "Uh, yeah. I have." God, it's like I'm a teenager again. I'm not a fan. "Well, I should get down there."

"Make sure you don't keep Mason waiting."

Yup, Grandma definitely knows we spent last night together. It's not a surprise, really. Like I said, the woman somehow knows everything. It's just embarrassing. How many other grandmothers know the frequency of their granddaughter's sex lives?

"You're late." Mason's sitting on the counter in the kitchen when I come in. "Not a very good hostess, are we?"

I playfully smack him and open the fridge to grab the eggs. "I thought you said you were helping? You could've started this, you know."

"You never told me what was on the menu," he says back. "As the guest, I think *I* have a right to know."

I roll my eyes with a smirk. "Well, now you know."

I hand him the carton of eggs. "Grab a bowl from underneath and whisk a couple of these together. We're making French toast."

He hops off the counter. "Bossy. I like it."

Cooking breakfast takes longer than usual, but it's also not a usual morning. Instead of eating in the dining room, we eat at the kitchen counter. Both of us chowing down off the same plate with the stack of toast.

"Hey, you're cutting into my side!" I give him a nudge. "Look at this pool of syrupy goodness here!"

"Keep it away from my powdered sugar. *That's* what real French toast needs!"

"No way!"

"Yes way."

"My house, my rules."

"But *I'm* the guest."

"Yes, but *I* made breakfast. Didn't your mother ever teach you not to bite the hand that feeds you?"

He reaches over and stabs into a small piece of toast slathered in syrup and dabs it on the end of my nose.

I wipe it away. "Hey!"

"You said you wanted syrup!"

Snatching the sifter filled with powdered sugar, I raise it above his head and try to sprinkle him with it, but he turns away before I can manage. Still, it gets all over his shirt.

"How's that for powdered sugar?" I ask triumphantly.

Mason dips his finger in the sticky plate and steps toward me. I back up around the kitchen island, giggling as he tries to rub his syrupy fingers on my face.

"What is this!" Grandma exclaims from the doorway.

We both stop in our tracks and look around. The egg shells are still sitting on a paper towel next to the bowl Mason whisked them in. There's egg and milk splattered on the counter next to the stove, which still has the skillet on it. And syrup and powdered sugar is smeared everywhere.

"My beautifully-cleaned kitchen!" she says, her hands on her hips.

"Sorry, Gram. We'll clean it up." I halfheartedly wipe some of the sugar from the counter onto my hand.

"You better!" She steps forward and pats Mason's shoulder. "Oh, not you, dear. You're our guest." She wipes away the sugar on his shoulder. "Although you should probably change."

"That's not fair!" I say with a grin.

"Hey, you heard her," Mason says. "Sorry I can't help. I *really* wanted to."

"Oh, well in that case," Grandma says. "The both of you can clean it up. After all, you two *never* have any time together."

I poke at the next piece of French toast and avoid any and all eye contact until Grandma's left the room.

"What was that about?" Mason asks in a low voice. "Does she know?"

"Yeah, probably."

His cheeks go red. "How?"

"She knows everything."

"That's...weird."

I smile. "That's Grandma."

The kitchen cleanup takes twice as long as it did to make the mess and once we've wiped every surface, washed all the dishes, and taken out the trash, the Parkers have arrived. They're a quiet older couple who seem very quiet. I must look like a freak still covered in syrup and sugar.

After I get them settled in and have run up to shower and change, I spot Mason outside on the back deck watching the ocean. Even though I can see the sweat dripping down his cheek from the kitchen, he's still in shorts and a T-shirt. Quite different from him lounging in swim trunks for most of his stay.

"Don't fall asleep!" I say loudly from the behind the screen door.

He jumps and gives me a scowl. "You're mean."

I walk over to him and he reaches for my hand. "I try. So what do you want to do today? Grandma gave me the green light to take the rest of the day off."

"Do you want to start planning your midsummer party while I'm still here?"

I consider it. It would certainly be helpful, but no. That would only serve as a constant reminder that he's leaving. "How about we go get ice cream and see where our feet take us?"

"How spontaneous of you," he says with a laugh.

The ice cream shop is just across the street from the Manor, but we continue walking until we wind up back at the park where he first kissed me.

Lying underneath the familiar oak tree, we stare up at the bright blue sky and talk. I learn more about his family. He has a younger brother who's going to school in the city for visual arts and is currently spending his summer backpacking through Europe. His parents have been married for almost thirty years—he also clarifies that he's twenty-eight, the same age as me. Six months younger, actually.

I tell him more about my time in New York City and even my life with my fiancé and some of the goals we wanted to achieve before it all came crashing down. But I don't spend too much time on that. Mostly, I talk about my grandma and how upset she was when my mother wouldn't move back down here after my grandpa died. Instead, Mom tried to get Grandma to sell the Manor and move to Virginia with her. Clearly, that didn't go over well.

We spend all day at the park, just lying side by side in the sun. The next day we do the same, and the day after that, until it's Mason's last day in Montana Beach. It doesn't even hit me that there are no more tomorrows like this until we get up at the park to head back to the Manor at the end of the day. This will be the last time I'll ever do this with Mason. The feeling weighs me down, both physically and emotionally.

"My grandma's probably got a whole party planned for you," I tell him as we make our way back home. It's the best I can do to try to keep the mood light, but my voice is hollow.

"She asked me what I wanted for my last meal," he says. "Made it sound so ominous."

"Yeah, she's a little dramatic." I stare at my feet as we walk hand-in-hand.

"She's been fun, though. This whole trip has been nothing like I was expecting—in a good way."

"I'm glad."

"Yeah."

We're quiet the rest of the way back. The Parkers

are at the Clinton's for dinner, so it's just the three of us who sit down to dinner. I can't decide if that's a good thing or not. By the time Grandma starts talking, though, I've decided it's not very good at all.

"Are you all packed up?" she asks Mason.

"Yes, ma'am."

She stretches her arm out and points across the table toward the front of the house. "There's a gas station right on the boulevard, just before you leave town. You'll want to stop there to fill up. Hopefully that'll take you a few hours north before you have to stop again."

He nods. "I will, yeah. On the way down, I managed to only have to fill up twice."

"Oh, that's great!" She cuts into her chicken. Grilled and doused with seasoning she must've picked up at the market. "I do hope you've enjoyed your stay. I know it's been a pleasure for both me and Jessie. Isn't that right, dear?"

"Huh?" I've only been half listening. Too busy in my own head wondering what the chances are that Mason will stay. He was considering turning down his father's offer, wasn't he?

But why would he? It's good money where his family is. I mean, he was able to take a whole month off and his father's paying for his brother to spend two months in Europe. With that kind of money, he'd be stupid to turn it down for someone he's only known a couple weeks. I'm not even going to bring it up.

"Jessie Girl, are you all right?" Grandma pushes.

"Uh, yeah." I set my fork down and wipe my mouth. "I'm just not very hungry. Sorry." I get up and carry my plate to the kitchen.

It feels like there's this pressure building up inside me. A growing overwhelming sadness that he's going, mixed with anger at myself for falling for him. Didn't I say that this wasn't going to be a summer fling? Why did I let it happen? How did I become attached so quickly?

I lean against the counter and fight back the tears that threaten to spill out of my eyes. I won't cry. Not in front of him, at least. Not until he's gone. He's still sitting in the next room. Crying about something that hasn't happened yet is just stupid.

"Jessie, dear, are you okay?" Grandma carries in hers and Mason's plates stacked on top of each other.

I suck in a deep breath. "I'm fine."

She gives me a sad smile. "Aw, honey. Who are you kidding?" She sets the plates down and pulls me into a hug. "I'm sad he's going, too. But mostly, I hate to see you like this again."

Pulling away, I shrug and say, "Well, no matter what I feel, he's leaving."

Grandma presses her hands on my cheeks to get

my attention. "If there's something you need to tell him, I think tonight's the best time to do it. If you want him to stay, tell him. He won't consider it unless you ask."

"Did he tell you that?"

She chuckles. "Oh, honey, he didn't have to! I've been around for a bit. I know everything. Remember that! Now, go upstairs and say what you need to say before you regret it."

She's right. Not that I should be surprised because she usually is. But I just don't know if anything I say will make him stay. It just doesn't make sense for him to. Still, with Grandma's insistence, I climb the stairs to Mason's room and knock, my heart rate quickening with each passing second.

He opens the door and leans against it. "Hey."

"Hey." I tuck some of my hair behind my ear. "Can I come in?"

"Sure."

He steps aside to let me in and I move right to the balcony. Any trace of the sun is almost completely gone for the night. This is it. His days in Montana Beach really are over.

"I guess I just wanted to talk to you about…" I turn and look at him, the tears threatening to fall once more. "I don't really know. I just wanted to see you, I guess."

He steps forward and takes my hands. "I'm glad

you did. I've been thinking about all of this over and over. I can't imagine driving off without you tomorrow. It makes me want to stay here."

My heart flutters with a glimmer of hope but my rational thinking quickly shoots it down.

"But my dad…" He trails off. "And it's not like you can come back with me. You can't leave Montana Beach."

We're quiet as we swing our interlocked hands between us. A distraction. Only the sound of the waves crashing fill the air until I quietly ask, "Would you consider staying?"

He doesn't say anything at first, but I can feel his eyes on me as I look down at our hands. "Would you want me to?"

I meet his eyes, the lump in my throat quivering my words. "Of course."

Mason leads me back inside and takes a seat on the bed. He pulls me closer to him. I lean down and kiss him once.

"You know how I feel about you," he says. "If I knew that you felt the same way, then my decision would be easy."

I pull my eyes away from his to study the bedspread. He wants me to tell him that I love him. Like that'll solve anything. As if professing my love will suddenly change the fact that he has a life in New York and I have one here. Like it'll make everything easy for him to uproot his life.

But it won't. I know that just because you love someone, it doesn't make everything okay. Life goes on. I learned that with my fiancé.

"Jessie," he pushes, "do you love me?"

Swallowing hard, I look over at the clock on the bedside table. Just after nine. "I should probably go. You've got a long day ahead of you tomorrow. You need your rest."

He sighs and gets up to walk me to the door. Just before he opens it, he looks at me with disappointment in his eyes and kisses me. "I love you, Jessie Ray."

Not sure if I can trust my voice, I simply nod and head out into the hallway. I race up to the apartment and am grateful that Grandma's not up here yet. I escape to my room and finally release the tears that have been building inside me.

My run is extra long this morning. I swear I could probably run all the way to North Beach and still not feel like I've gone far enough. By the time I get back to the Manor, Grandma's already served breakfast for Mason and the Parkers. She normally doesn't like it when she has to get everything ready all by herself, but she cuts me some slack today by not bringing it up.

I take my time to get ready, thinking that the longer I take, the longer Mason will stay. But after I've fussed in the mirror more than I normally do, Grandma calls to me from the balcony to hurry up.

Mason's leaving.

With the heaviness I've carried since we left the park yesterday, I trudge down the stairs to the front door. Mason's got his car keys in one hand and his sunglasses in another.

"You've got all your things packed in the car, then?" Grandma asks him.

"Yes, ma'am."

"Well, drive safe, dear." Grandma reaches up to give him a hug. "The month certainly flew by. Next time you're looking for a beach vacation, remember us."

"Oh, I definitely will. Thanks for everything. Take care."

"Not a problem," she says. "Just doing my job."

When they spot me, Grandma disappears into the kitchen, leaving just me and Mason.

"I don't know if we should even say goodbye," he starts. "That means that we'll never see each other again.

And we will, won't we?"

I shrug. "Sure. Maybe."

"Jessie, please don't be like this."

My shoulders slump and I step forward to wrap my arms around him, resting my face against his chest. I squeeze him tight. Even as he squeezes me back, I tighten my grip, imagining myself holding him in place. Right here in Montana Beach.

With me.

But he has to go. This isn't his home.

"I'll call you when I get back." He gives me a kiss.

"Drive safe," I mutter when we part.

He lingers. "I'll miss you, Jessie."

I nod, not trusting my voice.

"Goodbye," he says as he steps through the door. He gives me one last look and then turns the corner toward his car.

Just like that, he's gone.

I step out onto the sidewalk to watch him pull away, but the further he drives down the boulevard, the more I lose track of him.

Grandma steps out and puts her arm around me. "He's a special one."

"Yeah," I croak.

"Why don't you and I do something fun, huh? The Parkers will be gone for most of the day and the chores can wait. What do you say we go upstairs and play some cards? Or we can go on our own little day trip. How's that sound?"

I give her a sad smile. "Thanks Gram, but I just want everything to get back to normal. We have a lot of things to do before the party."

"Jessie, dear, it's okay to take a day off," she says. "I think you could use it."

"I'll be fine." I look out to the place I saw Mason's car last. I really don't know what normal is anymore. How can one person have that much of an effect on you in such a short period of time?

Chapter Ten:
MASON

Once I hit the open road after stopping for gas at the station Ethel pointed out, I immediately feel an emptiness inside me. It's a far cry from the complete relaxation I thought I'd feel when I finally made my way back home. Instead, my stomach is knotted up and it takes every ounce of strength in me not to turn the car around and go back to Montana Beach. Back to Jessie.

But I can't. I have responsibilities. I need to see my family. I do miss them. Maybe all I need to do is get back to my regular life and then I'll feel better.

The whole way home, all I can think about is Jessie, though. How beautiful she is. How strong she is. How much I wished this summer could stretch for eternity. Our time together was perfect.

Well, not exactly *perfect*, but memorable. Even when we had issues.

But this last week made up for those times. It proved how much I care for her. Even though I wanted our moments to last forever, it seemed to be over in a second.

The traffic congestion gets worse the closer I get back to the city. Getting closer to home doesn't help alleviate my loneliness. I drive more recklessly than I normally would, weaving between cars, and driving at a higher speed than usual. It's like the hollowness inside me is driving, pushing me to do things I wouldn't normally do. If I can't be with Jessie, then what's the point?

I know how ridiculous that sounds. Especially since the woman I love can't even say how she feels about me. Still, it's like I left a part of me with her.

The headlights flash across the neighboring house when I finally pull into the driveway back at my parents' house.

Home.

Except, this place now feels foreign to me. Even though I know this house, this street, this neighborhood like the back of my hand, it's like I'm a guest here.

"Paul! Paul, he's home!" Mom calls into the house as she comes out to greet me with a hug. She's wrapped in her bathrobe. "Oh, honey! I'm so glad to see you! Did you have a nice time?"

"Yeah, it was a lot of fun. Very relaxing," I say, squeezing her tight.

I decided on the way back that it's better to tell Mom about Jessie separately from Dad. Tell her how I'm torn about being back home. Maybe then she can help me determine where Dad's head's at and how to go forward to make things better for both of us. *If* there is a path forward.

"Welcome home, son!" Dad says when he emerges from the house in his boxer shorts and white tank top. He comes down the steps and hugs me, slapping my back hard. "How the hell you been, boy? Finally decided to come home, huh?"

"Yeah, I guess so."

"So have you decided, then? Are you going to take over for your old man?" he asks excitedly. No time wasted with him.

"Paul, let him come in and relax," Mom says. "I'm sure he's very tired from the drive."

"I just asked a question!"

She rolls her eyes and concedes, moving to the car to pull out my bag.

I try to cast her a look, but she's too preoccupied with my luggage.

"Do you want me to throw a load of wash in for you, dear?" she asks.

"No, I can get it, Mom. Don't worry about it," I say quickly.

"Well, let me bring it in for you, then," she says. "And don't you two stay out here too long. It's getting chillier each day." Hauling my bag over her shoulder, she walks up the few steps and disappears into the house.

I guess I'm not going to get a chance to talk to her separately before I give Dad an answer. I'm forced to give him one now.

"So, what is it, son?" he pushes with a smile. As if he already knows what I'm going to say.

"Dad, I just want to get some sleep. Can I decide in the morning?"

"Decide? What's left to decide? You had a whole month to decide! Don't tell me you need more time. I want to go into the office tomorrow and tell everyone the good news!"

I sigh and nod slowly.

I'm home, so why wouldn't I take him up on his offer? I need a way to earn a living and this is a very good one. Especially after taking a month off. "Yeah, Dad. I'll do it."

"Atta boy!" He pulls me in for another hug, slapping my back even harder. "That's right! That's my boy! I knew you wouldn't let me down!"

I give him a half smile.

"What's with the look?" He playfully taps his fist against my gut and I curl away with a forced laugh. "Hey, this is a big deal! Come on, let's get inside so we can both get some sleep. I'll give you one more day and then I expect you back at the office first thing, got it?"

"Yeah Dad, that works."

He hooks his arm around me as we walk inside the house and slaps my chest. "I'm real proud of you, son."

I thought a good night's sleep and waking up in my own bed would put me in a better mood but it's just another reminder that I'm not in Montana Beach anymore.

And it's not just that my summer vacation is over. Sure, I miss the beach, the sun, the small town, the slower pace, all of it. But I miss Jessie the most. And after I officially accepted Dad's offer last night, I know there's no turning back. The wheels are in motion to cement my life in New York while Jessie's is already firmly intact in Montana Beach.

By afternoon, I call Jessie since my parents are still gone and I know she will likely be done with most of her chores. Even though I just saw her yesterday, my heart rate quickens with each passing ring.

"Hello?"

"Jessie? It's Mason."

"Oh, hi! Did you make it home okay? How was your drive?" She sounds happy to hear me, which instantly brings a smile to my face. Good thing I'm alone.

"Yeah, it was fine. I slept forever, though." I force a laugh to try to hide how much I miss her.

"That's good."

"How's everything there? Did you get those new guests checked in?"

"Yup, they're actually out by the pool now."

"Oh gotcha." I feel a twinge of jealously that they're in my spot at the Manor. Lounging by the pool so that I can get a glimpse of Jessie as she does her chores.

"Yeah. Were your parents excited to see you?"

"Oh yeah. My dad was thrilled that I took him up on his offer, too."

"I bet." The cheerfulness in her voice is gone now.

"I start training with him tomorrow," I add, hoping that it'll spark further conversation.

"I'm sure you'll do great."

"I guess so, yeah."

"Are you happy?"

I shrug, knowing she can't see it. "I guess so. I haven't started yet, so—"

"Oh, I'm sorry, Mason. Grandma's calling me. I'm supposed to help her move some plants to bigger pots. I'll text you later tonight. Bye!"

The line dies and I click my phone off. I try to convince myself that Ethel really did need her help, but a part of me still worries that Jessie was just trying to get me off the phone. Maybe it's her way of coping with my absence. Either way, our conversation, no matter how brief, will likely be the highlight of my day.

Mom comes home with two shopping bags full of groceries. I help her unload the steaks and other fixings.

"Your father wants to grill tonight," she tells me. "Says that your homecoming deserves a celebration." She smiles at me. "Not that I disagree with him, but I'd rather not go broke on beef when one of our sons comes home. He better not insist on this again when your brother gets back from Europe."

"Is he coming home soon, then?" I ask.

"It's hard to say. Last we heard from him, he was in Switzerland and he needed to get back to Frankfurt in Germany to book a flight home," she says. "Then he could be on standby for a couple days."

I shake my head. "No thanks. I'd take my relaxing

vacation over that headache."

"Are you all ready for your first day back tomorrow?"

I shrug. "As ready as I can be."

Mom puts the meat in the fridge and folds up the shopping bag. "What's the matter?"

"I just miss everyone I met down there."

She touches the side of my face. "Well, sure, honey, you spent a month down there."

"There was someone in particular—"

"There's my newest apprentice!" Dad shouts from the front door. "Do I have a lot to tell you!" He comes in, kisses my mom, and then pats me hard on the back. "Get the grill fired up and I'll be right down to tell you everything!"

When he disappears upstairs to change, Mom asks, "What were you saying, dear?"

I brush it off. "Nothing. It's not a big deal."

We eat dinner outside at the picnic table on the tiny patch of grass that is our backyard. The neighbor's dog from three houses down barks loudly and the sound of other families outside can be heard from over the fence.

Dad catches me up on everything I've missed at the office in detail. Says that the whole team is excited to have me back and that he got started on the memo to the employees this morning explaining my new role.

Summer Stay

"Once we get you reacquainted from your little soul-searching trip, I can really start throwing the big CEO stuff at you," he says in between bites of his steak.

"That's great, Dad."

"Tell us more about your trip, honey," Mom says. "How was it?"

"Not now, Margie, we have to talk business first."

And he does. Until the sun sets behind the row of tightly-packed houses. He gives me what feels like every little facet of the firm from the last four weeks, reiterating again and again how happy he is that I'm going to follow in his footsteps.

The next day during my first day back at work, Dad announces my return to everyone and anyone we pass by in the halls and fills me in—again—about what's happened since I left.

By the time I get a moment to myself in my own office, it's almost three in the afternoon. My feet still haven't readjusted to the uncomfortable shoes, the sudden presence of a collar on my neck makes it sweat, and I generally feel worse about the direction my life is going now.

As I go through my day-to-day tasks, it makes it feel like my time in Montana Beach never actually happened. Like it was just a long, detailed, realistic dream.

I call Jessie again when I get home and try to sound cheerful. I tell her about my first day back at work and what it's like being home. With a lot of questions from me, she tells me a little about the new guests and some of the things she's planning for the midsummer benefit. But it takes a lot of effort on my part to get her to talk.

At dinner, Dad tells Mom all about my first day back at work. I try to sound enthused for his sake, but my heart's just not in it anymore. I left it back with Jessie at the Manor.

The routine quickly starts to wear on me. I wake up early each morning to go for a run just like I did at the beach, but watching the sun rise over the houses in my neighborhood isn't quite the same thing as watching it over the ocean. And I'm acutely aware of the fact that I'm running solo.

On my third day back in the grind, I help Mom dry the dishes after dinner. Dad is passed out in the living room in front of a rerun of *Seinfeld*.

We work in silence, only the sound of the TV in the next room fills the house.

"You're not happy," she says quietly, as if she knows it to be fact.

I take a plate from her and dry it. "Not really, no." No sense in lying to her.

"What's the matter?"

Setting the dish in the cupboard, I shrug the question off. "It's stupid."

"Not if it's upsetting you. You can tell me."

I take in a deep breath. "I met someone down there. Her name is Jessie and she—we had a really good time together, Mom. A *really* good time. I—" I stop myself from admitting just how deeply I feel for her. This is the first Mom's hearing of this girl. She's going to write it off as puppy love if I lead with that. "I didn't expect to miss her this much."

She gives me a sad smile and dries her hands before she hugs me. "Aw, honey. Is that who you've been talking to on the phone? I heard you in your room last night."

I look down to hide my embarrassment that she overheard. "Yeah. I don't think she's happy, either."

"Well, of course not. You two just spent four weeks together. It's going to take some adjustment to get back to normal. But things *will* get back to normal. Just give it time."

I shake my head. "But she's not the only thing that's wrong. Not really."

"What is it, then?"

Glancing over at the door to the living room, I see the flashing TV illuminate the room. Dad's feet are just visible through the doorway.

"I don't think I want to work for Dad anymore."

"Oh." She lets out a long sigh to buy time. "Why did you tell him you did then?"

"He kind of put me on the spot, didn't he?"

"I suppose he did." She turns back to the sink and picks up the sponge again. "But your father is very excited about you taking over for him. It's all he could talk about while you were gone and now that you're home, he's over the moon."

"I know. That's why this is so hard."

Mom shakes her head. "It's not hard. You made a promise to your father and you need to keep it."

"But this isn't just promising to spend a Saturday with him, this is my life. My future. If I take over for him, I'm stuck at the company until I retire — if Dad will even let me retire."

"Stuck? Honey, your father has worked hard to make the company a success. The company that has kept a roof over our heads and fed us your whole life. All he wants you to do is take his place so that it can continue to keep you fed with a roof over your head. This is just his way of making sure you're taken care of."

"But isn't it important to do what *I* want to do?"

"Yes, of course it is," Mom says curtly.

"I kind of want to quit."

She tosses the sponge in the sink and turns to me,

water dripping from her hands, faucet still running. Her eyes bore holes through mine. "If you quit, you're going to break your father's heart. Is that what you want to do to the man who just wants what's best for you?"

I don't say anything to that because I know she's right. It'd be a comfortable life with this job.

His job.

His life.

But what he has planned isn't what's best for me.

I trudge through the next day at work, sitting in on meetings with Dad, trying to decipher what it is he expects from me now that I'm his apprentice.

All the while, I'm thinking of what Jessie's doing at each moment. Is she cleaning up from breakfast? Watering the plants with Ethel? Running to the store for groceries for the guests? Cleaning the pool filters? Washing the sheets? What does she do once her chores are done? What does she do without me?

I wonder how many more guests have come to stay at the Manor. I wonder if she's feeling more confident about its future. Or if Mr. Tyson has finally backed off in his quest to buy it from them.

When I try to ask her all of this when I call her later that night, she doesn't really tell me much.

"Just the same guests I told you about."

"We're okay."

"I haven't heard from Mr. Tyson lately."

The rest of the call is very one-sided. I keep trying to come up with new ideas to strike up a conversation. Anything will do. That last week at the park, we talked about anything and everything. It was so simple. Easy. Now it seems forced.

Instead of getting angry with her about it, I let it go. She probably doesn't want to talk because of how much she misses me. She's always been so guarded, so why would she tell me that she wants me to come back when she couldn't even tell me how she felt before I left?

And I'm the one who left. I'm the one who has a new job to distract me. She doesn't. One minute we were inseparable, the next I was gone. It's different for her.

What's worse is that my new job isn't even distracting me anymore. I still feel hollowed out. Like I'm just going through the motions and not really enjoying anything that I'm doing.

By lunch time on Friday, I've made up my mind, even if it fills me with anxiety. In one conversation, my path will change from certain to unknown. And now, as I walk to my father's office, I'm trying my best to build up my confidence to tell him my intentions.

"Hey Dad, can I talk to you for a minute?" I pop my head inside his door.

He looks over his glasses at me and then turns back

to his computer. "Sure, son, come on in."

Closing the door behind me, I step behind one of the chairs opposite his desk and rest my hands against the back of it.

"Have a seat," he says.

"Uh, Dad, look, it's been a challenge to get back to work after being off for so long," I start. Definitely not the way I rehearsed it in my head, but I can't take the words back now.

"I bet. But you seem to be bouncing back just fine." He turns back to his computer.

"Well, I'm not so sure."

"Don't be so hard on yourself." He doesn't even look at me when he says it.

"No, Dad, I need you to listen to me. I don't think this is working out anymore."

That gets his attention.

"What do you mean?"

"I mean, I don't think this is the job for me anymore." There's a burning in the pit of my stomach that seems to grow the longer this conversation carries on. "It never really was."

"So what are you saying, son? You want to quit? Just like that?" His voice rises with each sentence. "Right after you told me and *everyone* else that you were going to take over for your old man?"

"Dad, this isn't —"

He leans forward across his desk and points at me. "No, Mason. You're not some punk kid who can just pop off for summer vacation whenever he wants. Now get back to your office and finish your work! Have you approved that artwork Fleetwood sent over yet?"

My hands shake, but I keep them on the back of the chair to steady them. "I'm not going to."

Dad pulls off his glasses and turns to me. "What are you trying to do? You understand I've already made arrangements for you to take over, right?"

"Look, I know how much you want me to be a younger version of you, Dad, but it's not who I am. It's not what I want to do. I hate it here."

"So what are you going to do instead? Run back to that beach town? Summer camp doesn't last forever, kid."

My anger reaches a boiling point and I want to throw this chair at him, but I push it all down inside. Instead, I just say, "I quit."

Chapter Eleven:

JESSIE

"Thanks again for hosting the event," I tell Adrian as I carry a case of liquor from the storage room to the bar. "I'm hoping the booze will draw people in."

He laughs. "I think it's just what you need. Sorry again I couldn't come to your Fourth of July party. I was a little busy that night." He takes the box from me and pulls out bottles to line the bar.

"Oh yeah?" I ask. "With a guy?"

He gives me a sly grin.

Planning the party with just me and Grandma was a lot of work, but Adrian's helped out as much as he could. For the most part, planning the fundraiser was a good distraction from Mason…except for the fact that all of my friends seem to be in the midst of their own summer flings as well.

They've asked about Mason, but I haven't really told them much. His absence is still too new. He's been gone for a week and even though I've stopped crying about him, I still miss him. And I'm still kicking myself for not telling him how I feel. I've considered telling him on the phone, but what would be the point? It's the same attitude I had when he left, too.

"What about you?" Adrian asks, breaking into my thoughts. "Have you heard from your guy?"

"Yeah, he's called a few times." I help him unload the last of the liquor from the case. "I don't know. I guess I'm just not into doing the long distance thing, so I don't really see the point in talking to him."

"Well after you bitch-slapped him here a couple weeks ago I'm sure he's probably feeling the same way."

I blush. "Tyler told you about that, huh?"

"Jess, *everyone* told me about that because they all saw." He breaks down the empty box.

"Yeah, yeah, yeah." I roll my eyes. "What about your guy?"

"What about him?"

"Tell me about him."

He gives me a look but doesn't say much more.

"So you're still mum about him?" I ask.

"You got it," he says.

"But when are we going to meet this mystery man?"

Adrian carries the folded box back to the stock room and I trail behind. "Oh, I don't know. He's kind of private. Not really out."

"Not really? What does that mean?"

"None of his friends or family know."

"But he's dating you…"

He pushes against the swinging door. "We were talking about *you*, I believe. So tell me, what's going on with this friend of yours?"

"Nothing anymore." I grab another case from the shelf and follow him out.

"But there *was* something, wasn't there?"

"Yeah, I guess."

He sets the case down on the bar. "Don't guess. You know. If you really care for him you'll work it out."

I set my case on the bar next to his but don't say anything more. I hope Adrian's right, but I just don't see how that's possible. Mason's life is heading in the opposite direction. He's already gone. He asked me several times to convince him to stay and I didn't. I gave him my answer on where we stood when I refused to say that I—

"Jessie Girl!" Grandma calls from the beach,

breaking into my thoughts. "Can I get your help out here?"

"Yeah, Gram?" I ask once I'm out on the beach in the setting sun. The party is supposed to start in two hours, once it's dark. Can't really have a bonfire in the daylight.

"The fellows who are dropping off the firewood are bringing their truck around," she says. "Be a dear and make sure it goes where it's supposed to go, will you?"

I nod. "Sure, no problem."

"Oh, and have you found someone to man the fire pit?"

"Yup, my friend Tyler will. He works here, too."

She raises her eyebrows. "And he's going to stay away from alcohol all night?"

"Mm-hmm. The fire department will be here, too, just in case."

"Oh good." She cups my face and says, "Thank you, dear."

"What are you up to?" I ask.

"Checking to make sure the food Marsha brought is all set."

Marsha's donated more burgers for the benefit. Even though the Nine serves food, I didn't want to take full advantage of Adrian, so we worked out a deal to split the profits of alcohol sales. That way he can still make some money with food sales once Marsha's stock runs out.

"Anything else you need help with?" I ask.

"No honey, I think I've got it under control. The Chinese auction is all set up and once I'm done in the kitchen I'll set up the check-in and donation table. We're almost ready to roll!"

Grandma insisted on a donation table by the front door where she'll be taking the cover fee to get in all night. Honestly, though, I wouldn't be mad if people just came from the beach to the fire. They'd likely go up to the bar and order a drink, which means we'd still be making money.

We've come a long way since our Fourth of July party. All on our own, too.

After I've made sure the firewood gets delivered okay and the fire department begins setting up the fire, I spot Tyler on the patio heading toward the beach and make sure he knows he's now officially on duty for the night. I head back inside to join Grandma at the donation table.

"Well, it's just about time." She checks her watch as she lingers behind the table near the entrance. "Hopefully we'll have a better turnout than our last party."

"We will," I assure her.

"We should've sold more tickets beforehand," she says.

"We'll be fine, Gram."

I gave tickets to the few businesses left in town and put up the flyers I printed at home basically *everywhere*. Hopefully the word got out. The last time I checked in on ticket sales, they were pretty good. If nothing else, we'll have made money from those.

"Uh, guys, did you unlock the door?" Adrian comes up from behind me. "There's a crowd lined up outside."

"Really?" I ask, surprised. I knew we'd have a good turnout, but I didn't think they'd be waiting to get in.

"Yeah." He goes to the door to open it and leads a long line down into the basement bar of the Nine.

"They can't *all* be from Montana Beach."

Adrian shrugs.

"They're not," a familiar voice says. "I *may* have helped with the advertising."

I turn around and my heart jumps as Mason steps into the bar from the beach.

Chapter Twelve:
MASON

Jessie takes a nervous step toward me and I wrap her in a hug, breathing in her hair, her skin, her being. The familiar burning sensation returns to my belly after being absent for the last week. It's all because of her. Finally, I'm home again.

Pulling myself away from her for a moment, I take her hand and lead her out onto the beach before the bar gets too crowded. Once we're outside, I look down at her to start to explain but she stretches up on her toes and kisses me. I wrap my arms around her again and hold her tight. God, I've missed this. I've missed her.

When we part, she looks up at me and asks, "What is this? Why are you here?" The ever-present smile on her face brings one to mine too.

"I've missed you, Jess," I tell her. "I drove all night to make it in time."

"I've missed you too. I honestly didn't think I'd ever see you again."

"I could tell from the way you've been on the phone."

She chews on her bottom lip. I love it when she does that.

"Yeah, sorry about that," she says.

"It's okay."

She takes my hands and looks up at me. "Mason, what are you doing here? You're supposed to be in New York. Did you decide not to take the job?"

"No, I did."

"Oh." Her smile fades and she starts to pull her hands away from mine, but I tighten my grip.

"I was miserable, Jessie. I was back at my parents' house and back at my old job, but it didn't feel right. It didn't feel like home anymore."

She looks down at the sand. "It's only been a week. Maybe you just needed longer to adjust."

"I hated it from the first day."

Her eyebrows scrunch together as she studies me. "I'm so confused. What are you doing here? Did you quit?"

I rock my head back and forth. "Yes and no."

"What does that mean?"

"It means I've got a few things in motion."

"Mason, just tell me. I can handle it."

I laugh. "Oh, you can?"

She rolls her eyes. "What are you going to do for a job now? That was your father's company. It's where your home is. Your family."

I shake my head. "Doesn't feel like home anymore."

"Oh." She studies me as she processes everything.

"Every night I would look forward to coming home and talking to you." I bring her hand up to my lips and kiss the back of it. "I could tell from our phone calls that you weren't happy, either."

"So did you quit? Mason, that was a steady job and—"

"It's not with you," I interrupt. "Jessie, none of that stuff really matters to me. It's how I ended up in Montana Beach to begin with. I knew in my gut that something in my life was off and that there was something bigger for me outside of the comfortable bubble I was living in. And I found the answer when I found you."

This makes her blush and divert her eyes again. After a moment, she punches me lightly in the chest. "Well, you don't have to turn into such a sap."

"Yeah, yeah." I roll my eyes with a smirk. "But listen, I shouldn't have tried to force you to say things you weren't ready to say. I'm sorry for that."

"Oh." She diverts her eyes again.

"Yeah. I should've just let you say it when you were ready, because I love you regardless —"

Jessie cuts me off with a kiss. It's the best way to be interrupted.

"No," she says when she pulls away. "I should've been honest with you."

The curiosity gets the better of me and I ask, "So why weren't you?"

She shrugs. "I don't know. I guess I was just scared. And I didn't want to be the person standing in your way of making an important decision. If you wanted to move back to New York and become a hotshot at your dad's ad firm, I wasn't going to stop you."

"Well, thanks for that sentiment, but it would've saved me a lot of time and money if you would've said that earlier!" I laugh.

"Sorry."

"Don't worry about it," I say. "I'm here now, aren't I?"

"Yeah."

I look into the bar at the burgeoning crowd that's working its way toward us. It's dusk and the bonfire crackles and pops not far from where we're standing. I don't want to ruin our reunion by talking about the future. It's terrifyingly exciting now. A feeling I've never really experienced.

"Should we head back to the party?" I ask.

"Not yet. There's something I need to say first."

"Jessie, I told you, when you're —"

"I do love you, Mason. And I wish I would've told you before, but I'm telling you now."

Even though I knew how she felt, even though I've imagined her saying it a million times since I first told her myself, it still takes me by surprise to hear the words out loud. To have her confirm what's only been inside my head all this time.

Wrapping my arms around her again, I pull her off her feet and kiss her as we both laugh.

"Hey lovebirds!" someone calls from inside.

I set Jessie down and look over to see half a dozen people staring at us.

"Adrian," Jessie mutters as she waves at him. She tucks some of her hair behind her ear, embarrassed.

"Get in here, there's someone who wants to talk to you," he calls to her.

I follow Jessie inside. She meanders through the crowd back to the front table. Ethel is talking to a middle-aged woman with curly blonde hair.

"Oh, there you are, Jessie Girl." Ethel wraps her arm around her granddaughter. "Hello, Mason. Are you all settled in, then?"

"Yes, ma'am," I say.

Jessie looks between us with a confused look, but Ethel motions to the curly blonde. "You know Patty Moore, right? She's the mayor of Montana Beach."

"Of course, yeah," Jessie says with a smile. They shake hands and she adds, "Glad you could make it. Thanks for coming to support us."

"Are you kidding? Local businesses supporting other local businesses right in the heart of town is exactly the kind of thing the village board and I have been trying to encourage for a while now," Patty says.

"Oh good!" Ethel chirps.

"And we have a petition going," Jessie says, pointing to the clipboard on the check-in table.

Patty leans over to look at the list.

"We already got most of the residents to sign it when we invited everyone to our Fourth of July party," Jessie says.

The mayor looks up at Jessie and smiles. "This is fantastic. Good job!"

"Thanks. I just hope—" Jessie stops midsentence when a familiar man in a black business suit comes down the stairs from the street.

"Is this where I pay for a ticket?" he asks Ethel.

"Hi, Mr. Tyson," Jessie says. "You remember my grandmother Ethel and my friend Mason?"

"Oh, *you're* Mr. Tyson," Patty says. She extends her hand and says, "Patricia Moore, mayor of Montana Beach. We talked on the phone, remember?"

"Oh, hi. How've you been?" he asks.

Patty brushes him off quickly with a smile and pulls him out of the queue. "Oh, just fine. Listen, I've been meaning to get back in touch with your office, but now that you're here I can tell you in person. It was decided at the last board meeting that the village is no longer interested in taking possession of Montana Manor."

"Oh? Why not?"

"Well, we've decided it's probably best not to drive out current businesses in the hopes that a new one will come along," she says.

"Now, I mean no disrespect, Ms. Moore, but I want to urge you to reconsider. That site is the most prime location in the village, situated at a major intersection right on the beach. It would be the perfect location for the business proposal I sent to your office."

She nods. "And that proposal was quite impressive. But, as you've said, the location of Montana Manor is an important one in the village. We wouldn't want just anything to be built there. It needs to be something that looks good and helps capitalize on the village's assets."

"Ms. Moore, if you're suggesting that a failing business would do better than—"

"Look around you, Mr. Tyson," she says loudly. "All of these people are here to support Montana Manor. It means something to us as a community. A community I once thought was gone, but now see that I was seriously mistaken."

"Now, Ms. Moore—"

Could he call her *Ms. Moore* any more?

Patty puts up her hand to stop him. "I know what you're going to say: that the village could use the money generated from your proposed tower, and I'd have to agree with you. We certainly *could* use the money. But as mayor, it's my job to also pay attention to what we might lose if we make the wrong decisions. Montana Manor is not something this community should lose."

He fixes the lapels of his jacket and says, "All right, then. Well…I guess that's that."

I look over at Jessie and we smile at each other. It worked out. All of our hard work and determination paid off. Well, Jessie's hard work. She saved the Manor.

"I hope you stick around to enjoy the party," Patty tells Mr. Tyson.

"Oh, and don't worry about the five dollar entry fee," Ethel adds.

He takes another look around and then rubs the back of his neck. Clearly, he's not used to being turned down.

"No, I should probably get going," he says. "I wasn't planning on coming anyway. I just thought it was odd to see such a large crowd here. Usually it's empty."

Just had to get in the final jab. Based off what I saw the last time I was at the Nine, he's completely lying.

Patty leads him back to the stairs to the sidewalk. "Oh, I wouldn't expect you to be up to date on everything going on in town anyway. Not with how busy you are doing…something."

Damn, Blondie's got some jabs of her own!

She waves to him. "Good evening, Mr. Tyson. As always, it was a pleasure."

He scowls at the rest of us before climbing the stairs back to the street.

"That was awesome!" Jessie says when Patty rejoins our group. She gives her a big hug. "Thank you!"

Ethel makes a fist and says, "You really showed him!"

"Yeah, well, our problems in Montana Beach certainly haven't gone away, but you ladies have shown that they're not as dire as we thought." Patty looks out at the crowd. "Events like these will help restore a sense of community and encourage even more new businesses here."

"It will," I say. "And the fact that you're saving the historic buildings counts for something too. It keeps the character of the town."

"Very true, Mr. Wagner," she says.

Jessie looks between us, confused. "How do you—"

"We spoke on the phone," I tell her.

"How—what—*huh*?"

We laugh and I lead Jessie back out to the bonfire, which has a bigger crowd around it now that the sun has really set. There's music blaring from the speakers on the Nine's patio where several people dance. For everything going on, it's actually not too loud out here.

We take a seat in the sand and watch as the embers burn at the bottom of the fire.

"So what's going on?" Jessie asks. "Are you staying?"

"Yeah."

"How? I mean, you're not working for your father, but how is that going to work if you don't have a job?"

I lean back on my hands and pretend to consider.

"Well, I've got this sweet room to stay in at the best place in town. Beautiful views of the ocean, right on the beach."

"Wait, you already moved back to the Manor? Is that what Grandma meant earlier?"

I nod with a smile.

"How? I didn't see your transaction come through. When did you arrange that?"

"Well, I had to sleep in my car last night, but I called as soon as I woke up this morning. It was early. I figured you'd be out on your run. When I got through to Ethel, I made the arrangements with her. Checked in this afternoon after you'd already come down to set up. I wanted to surprise you."

"Well, you did!" She smacks my arm.

"Anyway, your grandma set me up in my old room. I dropped my stuff off just before I came down here. Your friend Tyler let me sneak into the storage room until the moment was right."

"Well, I'm happy about that." She picks up a clump of sand and lets it sift through her fingers. "But what are you going to do after tonight's over? How are you going to make a living? Aren't you going to want to go back to New York?"

"Nah," I shake my head. "After spending a month here, New York is too busy for me."

D. Allen

"But what about a job? There aren't any advertising agencies down here."

"Isn't there?" I ask.

"What?" Her eyes search my face for answers.

"My dad and I came to a compromise. He agreed to let me open up an office down here. I'll need to go up to New York frequently, but this is where I'll live. I've already arranged it with a landlord for office space and worked out an agreement with the village to get some money to clean up the building. It's going to take some work, but I can do it. This way, I'll still be working for my dad and I still get to be with you."

She smiles. "Really?"

"Yeah. Which means, I can help you and Ethel advertise the Manor. The whole village, really."

She looks away again. "We don't have any money to pay you, though."

I shake my head. "I'll need a place to stay. We'll work something out."

"That we will." Jessie rests her head against my chest.

I look up at the stars. They seem endless, just like the possibilities for the future. I don't have all the answers, but I have someone by my side to help me figure it out. We'll get there.

PICK UP **SUMMER JOB**, THE NEXT BOOK IN THE **MONTANA BEACH** SERIES AND LET THE SUMMER CONTINUE!
DAVIDNETHBOOKS.COM/MONTANABEACH

BEHIND THE BOOK:

Summer Stay

I've had the idea to write a summer-themed series for a while now, but I've always had other books to write in the meantime. I knew I wanted to write three books at once and have them intertwining so I needed several months between projects to write it.

My main goal with this series, specifically this book, was to portray a pure summer feeling. The one we all had when we were younger when we'd wake up in the morning and have a whole unplanned day ahead of us to do whatever we wanted. It was this simple, carefree, and relaxing tone that I wanted to use as the basis for not only *Summer Stay*, but the fictional Montana Beach in general. A slower-paced town that's been forgotten. After my more intense Fuse series, I needed to work on something with a lighter feel to it.

For the most part, this series was written in January 2018 and through the very cold spring that followed. I had originally plotted out the book in between drafts of *Oblivion*, the final Fuse book. I knew I wanted the structure and tone of the story to match my first romance title, *A Christmas Reunion*, but when I sat down to actually write *Summer Stay*, I had a different take on where I wanted the story to go.

In the initial draft, Mason was a party boy who comes to Montana Beach with a group of friends and when he meets Jessie, he starts to straighten out his ways. But then I asked myself: why would someone like Jessie *ever* go out with a party boy like Mason 1.0? Also, Grandma Ethel wasn't in the story at all. Jessie just ran the inn by herself and basically had no help or anyone to bounce ideas off of. I had planned on having her confide in Robyn a lot, but I was afraid that would intertwine their stories too much.

So I rewrote the plot, made Mason a guy who has his shit together (to be bluntly) and added Grandma Ethel not only as a source of counsel for Jessie, but also a bit of comedic relief. Hopefully that came across well.

The new outline worked so much better and I ended up writing the first draft in a week. With long chapters too. Nothing seemed forced and I was actually having fun writing it. This was the beach equivalent of my Small Town Christmas series.

The next problem I had, even after I wrote the series, was coming up with a good title. I'm horrible at titles (even though I think I've done a good job of coming up with them so far for my books) so I knew this would be a challenge. My original idea was to come up with something summer-themed for each book in the series. So an activity or something that is synonymous with the warmer months in the year. But I also wanted it to tie in well with the story.

The first idea I came up with was "Sink or Swim." I figured it worked with the story because Mason spends a lot of time at the Manor's pool and the inn was going to either be successful or it wasn't. I wasn't completely sold on that title and I wanted each book in the series to start with the same letter (I know, not really important, but it's what I wanted).

That's when I came up with "A Summer Stay." I liked the way the Small Town Christmas series was named so each book is titled, *A Christmas [Fill in the blank]*. Only, I didn't like that it matched *so* much, so I dropped "A" from all three titles and simply named it *Summer Stay*.

Since Montana Beach is a fictional town (named by my readers!), I decided it'd be best for my own sanity to map out the town so when I refer to things in the series, I'm consistent. Plus, I just like looking at/making maps! I had previously made a map for Olympia, which was the fictional city in my Fuse series, and I had a lot of fun making it. The only problem was, it was all hand-drawn and therefore couldn't go in the book. So with Montana Beach, I made the map on my computer.

I hope you enjoyed this book! I view my Small Town Christmas books as being similar to Hallmark Christmas movies and I wanted the Montana Beach series to be the summer equivalent of that. Hopefully that's the same feel you got from it too. I hope you enjoyed it anyway!

Please consider leaving a review online to help other readers decide if this book is worth a read. It would be a huge help!

— D. Allen
(JUNE 2018)

When Robyn was promoted to manager of the Montana Beach Pier amusement park, she helped save it from near extinction. But her employees are still having a hard time adjusting to her new leadership role. With her father gone and only a few friends in Montana Beach, the stress at work carries over to the rest of her life. That is, until her newest employee steps through the door.

Jaden's just looking for a summer job until he can find something more stable in the fall. Montana Beach might be a slower pace than his hometown, but his new boss and the romance that sparks between them makes the sleepy little town exciting.

When a coworker discovers their relationship, he threatens to reveal their secret, which could put their jobs and the future of the Pier at risk.

—MONTANA BEACH—
BOOK 2

D. ALLEN

Read on for an excerpt of the next book in
the Montana Beach series!

Chapter One:
ROBYN

My alarm wakes me at six in the morning. It's the first day of work this season at the Montana Beach Pier amusement park. Or just the Pier, as everyone calls it. I don't have to be at work for another five hours, but I want to squeeze in some painting time before the day gets started.

With my eyes slits from the cruel bathroom light, I brush my teeth before hopping in the shower, readjusting to my familiar routine from last summer.

I wish I could say I'm excited about starting the season again. I mean, I guess I am, but that's more to see the families stroll through the gates again. The kids are always so excited and they usually don't know which ride to try first. And then, by the afternoon, they're so hyped up on sugar and their parents are so drained from the sun that it makes for hilarious entertainment, even though I'm technically working.

But the door won't open to guests for another week. In the meantime, my employees and I have to get everything up to snuff for opening day. Which means they'll be cleaning up the rides after the maintenance guys check to make sure they're running okay and I'll be stuck in the office doing paperwork and getting our marketing materials together.

I step out of the shower, wrap a towel around myself, and walk into the second bedroom I use as part walk-in closet, part art studio. I don't have too many clothes, but I do have more than the tiny closet in my bedroom would allow. Still, there's enough space for my art supplies too. And all the paintings that are waiting to be sold. The perks of living alone, I guess. Anyway, I'm going to miss spending all day to paint the landscapes from around town, but I'll squeeze in time to keep painting when I can.

As I pick out clothes to wear, I try to remember everything I have to do when I go in today. I made a couple trips to the Pier office last week to start getting some paperwork started. I also hired two new people: a cleaner and a concession person, bringing our total number of employees up to fifteen. Including me. Not a lot, but it works.

Actually, I have another interview today. If he seems sane enough, I think I'll make him a ride operator. Out of the two other new employees, one is barely old enough to work, meaning I don't feel comfortable putting him in charge of a ride for kids under ten, and the other doesn't seem to even *want* a job, so I stuck her as a cleaner.

It seems mean, but that position is the easiest to make up for if we lose someone midseason. The guy I'm interviewing today might even spend half his shifts cleaning. We don't have the budget to hire too many designated cleaners, so everyone has to chip in.

Once I'm showered and dressed, I return to the spare bedroom and really look at my work in progress. It's starting to come together. I squeeze out some paint, dab in a brush, and get to work.

Usually I like to paint in the midst of my inspiration. *Plein air*, as it's called in the art world. It helps me really get in touch with my surroundings, but since I don't have a lot of time now that I'm working, I have to make do with a photo hanging on the wall above the canvas.

I work for a couple hours, filling out the canvas with more colors, bringing to life the sunrise scene that fills me with so many happy memories. Before I know it, it's just after ten and I rush to clean up my paints in the bathroom sink that's stained with colors from previous paintings; a work in progress itself.

Once I'm all cleaned up, I grab my bag and my keys and walk down to Atlantic Street, where there's a tiny little coffee shop on the corner with First Street.

"You're here early," Nancy says from behind the counter. "Your usual?"

"Yes, please," I respond. "It's my first day back at the Pier."

"Is it that time of year already?" She fills a to-go cup with a dark roast blend.

"Sure is. Creeps up faster each year."

"And passes by just as quickly!" She chuckles, passing me my order. "Here you go, dear."

I take the cup from her and hand her my card. "Maybe next year we'll be able to expand the season a bit, but I still need to whip my employees into shape. I've got a few new ones this year."

"I'm sure you'll be able to, honey. I'll have to bring my granddaughters down if I have time this year."

"Oh yeah! That would be fun!" I take my card back and slip it in my wallet. Slinging my bag back on my shoulder, I head to the door. "Thanks, Nancy. Have a good day!"

"You too, dear!"

My assistant manager, Peggy, is already in the office when I get to work. She's never early, so I must be a few minutes late. She has her feet up on the desk and is filing her nails while she snaps her gum.

"Sorry I'm late," I mutter. She probably doesn't care.

"Oh, you actually came back this year."

"I just knew it would make your day." I boot up the computer and take a sip of my coffee.

"I see you still haven't found a real job," she says.

"And neither have you," I say as polite as I can.

This is our relationship each summer. Verbally jabbing each other under the veil of a joke. I think she might want me to quit, but it's not like the owners would make her manager. They live up in North Beach and own several attractions up there. This tiny little pier all the way down in Montana Beach isn't on their radar too much, but they're still funding our operations, so that's good. I can imagine the attractions up north are making a lot more money than we are, though.

If they're forced to hire a new manager for the Pier, it might be easier for them to just close it. That's where it was heading before I started. I trimmed the budget, beefed up policies, and started advertising to the right audience. In the three years that I've had the position, the annual number of visitors has gone up by thirty percent.

Of course, in the process of turning this place around, I had to lay a few people off, argue with the remaining employees about my new policies, and took on the reputation of *bitch*. Collateral damage for saving a small town business.

The intercom beeps and I look up to the camera and see some of the workers down by the gate.

"Peggy, can you let them in? I'll meet you guys out in the break room in a few minutes for the meeting."

She sighs loudly, but drops her feet to the floor and steps out of the office. I take another gulp of my coffee, nearly burning my tongue. It's worth it. It would be a long summer without it.

I gather my notes and step into the next room where everyone's putting away their belongings before they begin the day. I do a quick headcount. Still waiting on a few people. Everyone's supposed to be working today because I didn't schedule a full day of hours. I also wanted to be able to have a meeting with everyone at once.

I do my best to smile and welcome everyone back, but most people don't seem to have much enthusiasm. It's still early. They're just tired. Yeah, that's it. A lot of people have coffee with them. I shouldn't have left mine on my desk.

Once the rest of the crew arrives, I clear my throat to get their attention, but they all still talk loudly to one another.

"Hey!" Peggy shouts. She's standing off in the corner, still filing her nails.

Slowly, the room quiets as everyone turns to face me.

"Thank you. Well, welcome back for another season, everyone! We have some new faces here, so for starters, everyone please welcome Michael." I motion to him in the corner. He's a relatively quiet guy. Judging by his baby face, I'd say he's right around eighteen years old. "He will be working concessions. Our other new employee is Julia." She's sitting on one of the benches next to Peggy. Her blonde hair is pulled away from her face in a French braid. "She'll be working with Anthony this year to keep the Pier looking nice."

Only a few people look in their direction. The rest seem bored.

"All right, we have a lot to do today, but I need to take a moment to discuss one thing in particular. Some of you came in after your eleven o'clock start time. Now, I know it's the first day of the season and you're probably trying to get back into the routine, but let's make an effort to be on time tomorrow, okay?"

Ugh, I hate doing that. I know it just feeds right into the image that I'm a bitch, but it's the first day and the same people are late again. Not much changes around here, apparently.

"All right, so today—"

Someone with dark scruffy hair raises his hand in the back. Max Sherman. He was among those who showed up late. He always is. Actually, he's the worst. I shouldn't have asked him back, but I was desperate for employees.

"Do you have a question?"

"Yeah, what does it matter if we're late or not?" he asks. "It's not like there's people lining up outside. I didn't see anybody out there, did you guys?"

The room laughs and some people even respond with things like, "Haven't seen anyone here in years," or "Surprised this place is even still open."

Even if they haven't seen the numbers, they must know there's been more guests each year. It's kind of hard to miss for such a small amusement park.

I wait until the room settles down again and then address Max directly. "We usually start working a week before the Pier opens to get it ready for opening day, but with your attendance record, I'm not surprised that you didn't know that."

The room erupts again, this time with comments like, "Ooo, she got you, man!" or "Damn, boss lady's got jokes!"

"Anyway," I continue loudly to silence them. "You've all received an email with a checklist of everything we need to get done before the park opens—"

"What email?" Max asks.

"The one that went out a couple weeks ago."

"Oh that? I must've thought that was junk." He laughs.

Man, I wish I had more coffee this morning. "Next time, be more careful, please. Basically, what I said in the email was that the owners are sending in maintenance people today to make sure the rides run fine after the winter. What we need to do is get everything else opened up. That means sweeping, waxing, pulling out picnic tables and benches from storage, stuff like that. It's going to take time, but working together we can get it done."

Max chuckles.

"Is there a problem?"

"No, I just thought I was watching an after-school special all of a sudden."

More laughs. I'm about to snap at them, but everyone's attention turns to the guy standing in the doorway. Maybe it's because he's new. Maybe it's because he's the only one not in the Pier's uniform of blue polo and khaki shorts. Or maybe it's because his smile could change anyone's attitude. But the room goes silent when he steps in.

"Hi, sorry. The gate was open and—I didn't mean to interrupt. I'm Jaden. I'm here for an interview."

"Good luck," someone mutters.

I shoot a glare in their direction and a few people recoil. This is definitely *not* the way I wanted to start the season off.

Softening my tone, I turn back to Jaden and nod in the opposite direction. "Why don't you take a seat in the office and I'll be with you in just a sec?"

He nods and walks past me to the open door. When he's out of sight, I turn back to my employees.

"Look, I don't want to have to be the mean boss, but you guys leave me no choice. Our customer attendance has been up in recent years, but we won't get more people in here if we don't each take a more active role in making sure they have a good time. That starts with *all of us* having a good time. Don't get in the mindset that this place is horrible. Yes, it's a job, but we can have fun with it. Our attitudes will reflect on the guests and keep them coming back. That means we'll all be here again next year and the year after that. Okay?"

To my surprise, I see a couple people shrug and

nod. That's probably the best I'll get from these guys for right now. I'll take it.

"Okay, then. Let's get to work. Peggy, can you assign jobs for everyone while I meet with Jaden?"

She takes the clipboard from me and leads everyone outside.

I take a deep breath in the silence that follows and return to the office. Jaden looks up and smiles when I enter.

"Sorry about that." I extend my hand to him. "I'm Robyn, nice to meet you."

"Jaden," he says.

I take a seat behind the desk. "Just give me a minute to get organized here." I search for his application. I know I printed it last week when I was in. "So tell me a little about yourself."

"Well, uh, I just graduated college, I'm staying in Montana Beach this summer, and I'm looking for a summer job."

I dig through a stack of papers in the corner. I told Peggy to file these, but I guess it didn't fit into her schedule.

"Uh-huh." I'm not really listening, too busy looking under papers and in drawers for his application.

"Yeah. I've done some retail in the past, but never anything like this," he says.

Summer Job

Finally, I spot it still sitting in the printer and snatch it. I skim it and ask, "So you're done with school, then?"

"Uh—yeah, I am."

It sounds familiar and I scrunch my nose. "You just told me that, didn't you?"

He smiles. "Yeah, but that's okay."

"Sorry about that. I've been so frazzled with the opening that I'm not all here just yet. Anyway, so now that you're done, what are you hoping to do full-time?"

He shrugs. "I don't know. I'm just looking for something for the summer right now and then hopefully find something fun in September."

"Something fun," I murmur as I scan his application again. There's a retail job at a tourist store listed and a work study job, which must be from when he was in college, but not much else. "What did you do at your retail job?"

"I was a cashier, so I was kind of the face of the customer service for the store. It's a small place, so there were really only two of us working at a time. If a customer needed help and my coworker was busy, I kind of acted like a personal shopper."

I nod. "Oh, nice. We need great customer service at the Pier. So I take it you're good with money?" Not that he'd actually be dealing with money much here, but it's better to ask more questions than not.

"Oh yeah. My drawer was always spot on."

"Excellent." I skim the brief description he has for his work study job. "It looks like you worked for a photographer in college."

"Yup. I was basically his assistant. Setting up shots in the studio, adjusting the lighting, I even developed a few photos myself in the dark room."

"How cool. That must've been fun."

"Yeah, it was."

I hate doing short interviews, but there isn't a lot more to ask. He's had customer service experience, which is huge with us in order to get customers to keep coming back. This position isn't exactly rocket science. I just want to know I'm not hiring a jerk like Max.

"Where are you from?" I ask, just to draw out the interview longer.

"North Beach, but I'm staying over on Cemetery Street this summer, so transportation won't be an issue."

"What made you want to come to Montana Beach?"

"It's quieter."

I chuckle. "That it is. Sometimes too quiet. But luckily, this place is the epicenter of activity in town each summer."

Summer Job

"That's good. I figured it's a nice change of pace here, too."

"A lot slower of a pace."

He smiles. "Just what I'm looking for."

I cluck my tongue as I search his application for another question. I've pretty much exhausted my questions. He seems like a hard worker and there aren't any other applications in the system to review. *This* is the reason I have the types of employees that I do.

"What's your availability?"

"Immediately," he says. "I could start right now if you really wanted."

My eyes snap up from the paper. "Could you?"

"Are you offering me the job?"

I flash him a smile. "I guess I am. You're hired."

Chapter Two:

JADEN

"I'm going to stick you with Max for today," Peggy tells me as we walk down the length of the pier. I've never been here before, but it seems like a cool place. Everything looks older than the amusement park in North Beach, but it's almost vintage now. The most notable thing here is the Ferris wheel, which sits at the end of the pier overtop of the water. I can only imagine how windy it can get up there.

"What do you want me to do?" I ask. Robyn said she had some paperwork to take care of in the office, so she asked Peggy to get me acquainted with everything.

"We're cleaning," she says. "It's not rocket science. The folks who have been here the longest are cleaning and waxing the rides. You can help Max sweep and mop the deck and pick up any trash you see laying around. Make sure you're thorough." She hooks her thumb back to the office building. "Boss Lady in there nitpicks everything."

I nod. "Sounds easy enough."

There's a kid with shaggy hair at the end of the pier sweeping the deck when we approach. Max, I assume.

"Hey, I'm giving you a shadow today," Peggy tells him. "Don't do anything stupid. Show him what needs to be done and have him help."

"For how long?" Max asks.

She shrugs. "All day, I guess."

He groans and she takes that as her cue to walk away, which leaves me standing there awkwardly when he resumes sweeping.

After a few seconds he points back down the pier. "There are some brooms in the storage room. It's the door on the right of the office."

I nod and go retrieve a broom. When I return, Max is leaning on his broom, looking out at the water. Not wanting to say anything stupid, I start sweeping where it looks dirtiest.

"So you're the new guy, huh?" he asks.

"Yup," I say, still sweeping. "I'm Jaden."

"Max." He turns around to look at me. "I didn't mean for it to sound like I didn't want you hanging around. She just always has an excuse to have eyes on me."

"Peggy?"

He shakes his head. "No, Robyn."

"Oh, she doesn't seem so bad," I say. "Kinda cute, actually. This summer could be fun with girls like her around."

"*Cute*? You think Robyn's *cute*?"

I drop my head down again. "Guess not."

"Look, whatever she's got going for her will be quickly overlooked once you get to know her. She can be a real bitch. Makes working here a living hell sometimes."

Seems nice enough to me. "I'll have to watch out for that."

He leans in closer and drops his voice. "The moment you do something wrong"—he snaps his fingers—"you're put on her shit list."

"I've had some bad bosses before. I'm sure I can handle it." So far, Robyn's not like any of them.

He starts sweeping again, pushing his pile over the edge of the pier. "What made you want to work here anyway?"

"Thought it could be fun," I say. "It's not quite as hectic as North Beach down here."

"Is that where you're from?"

I nod. "Yeah. It's basically tourist city. Figured I could spend a summer in a quieter place like this."

"Montana Beach is basically dead," Max says.

"I don't know about that. It's tiny, that's for sure, but there seem to be quite a few people who live here."

"Have you noticed there's only one place to stay in town? Unless you want to rent a house, but that can get expensive. Still, there's enough of them."

"Yeah, I'm renting one of the houses, actually."

"You are?" He wipes the surprise from his face. "Rich parents?"

I shake my head. "No, just working here. It *is* expensive, but I'll be just able to squeeze it. Actually, the house has two bedrooms, so if I had a roommate, I could split the cost."

His eyes grow wide. "Really?"

I shrug and push the growing pile of dirt in front of me. I don't want to push it over the edge. I might be new here, but I know that that's just lazy. "Yeah. It's not a big house, but it's nice. Not too far from the beach, either."

"Well, nothing in this town is too far from the beach."

"True."

"I've been meaning to get out of my parents' house for a while now," he says. "I would love to have my own place. I'm jealous."

I know what he's looking for and even though I don't really know him, I should probably find a roommate sooner than later if I'm going to be able to use any of the money I make working here on things *other* than the bills. Max has got a job and it's only for the summer.

"You could stop by after work and check it out if you're interested in taking the extra room at my place. It's a nice house."

He smiles. "Awesome, I definitely will. You mind if I hitch a ride with you?"

I shake my head. "I don't have a car here, but it's only over on Cemetery Street. We can walk."

"Oh, well that kind of sucks, but I guess it's not too far. Thanks, man!" He holds out his hand and I clasp it and give him a quick pat on the back.

"Looks like you two are getting along pretty well," Robyn says as she comes around the towering Ferris wheel.

"I was just showing him everything we need to do to open." Max quickly resumes sweeping, moving faster to get away from Robyn.

"Do you mind if I steal him for a bit?" she asks him, pointing to me. "I want to give Jaden the grand tour."

Max scoffs. "Okay, see you in five minutes."

Robyn ignores him and leads me around the

corner. "Well, obviously this is the Ferris wheel. It's the oldest attraction on Montana Beach Pier and the only one open to adults as well as kids. It has survived wind storms, hurricanes, and even a little bit of snow."

"No lightning?"

"Well, I'm sure it's been struck a few times," she admits. "But not since I've been here."

"How long's that been?"

"This is my third year as the manager. I was a ride op for several years before that, though."

"What's my position?"

Her eyebrows jump up in surprise. "Oh, I'm sorry! I never told you. I'm going to train you to be a ride op too, so you'll be one of the people in charge of running the rides."

I look up nervously at the Ferris wheel. "Are you sure you can trust a newbie with that? What if I go too fast and kill someone?"

Robyn rolls her eyes. "Nobody's died here. But if you did, that would at least get us some publicity." She smiles to show she's joking.

I laugh. "That's so bad."

"I'm kidding, obviously. No, the controls are pretty easy. It's basically all automated now, just as long as you press the right buttons and wait until you get the all-clear signal from your coworkers. We'll have Bailey or

Mackenzie or someone train you and you can shadow them until you get comfortable with it. You'll be fine."

"That shouldn't be so bad, then." I follow her over to the next ride, a long kiddie roller coaster. Each car is painted to look like ladybugs.

"This one is the most popular kiddie ride here, although it breaks down a lot of the time because it's so old. It's been here since the seventies, I think."

"Oh wow. Time for an upgrade." The metal fence surrounding the ride is rusted with a few rungs missing.

"I wish we could upgrade, but the owners haven't given us any extra money for repairs or replacements."

"Why not?"

She shrugs. "We're small fry compared to what they've got going on up in North Beach. You probably know what I'm talking about, right?"

I nod. "Yeah, there are a million different gimmicky entertainment venues. It's crazy up there."

"That it is."

Robyn takes me throughout the rest of the Pier and points out the other rides. There's a kiddie Ferris wheel for those too afraid to go on the big one. They also have a carrousel, a few midway games, and a stage where they try to get people to come and entertain.

"It's been getting harder to get people to come do a show for the kids," she admits. "But I think I have it booked up for most of the summer. That'll buy us some time to book the rest of the season."

The stage butts up against the Pier's office. The curtain the workers are reinstalling looks worn and torn, the stage itself looks flimsy, and there's nowhere for anyone to sit.

"Looks like this could use an upgrade too," I note.

She nods. "And I'm sure we'll get more money to upgrade everything as soon as we start making more money. It's kind of a catch-22."

"I can see that."

"So you're catching on that we're doing the best we can with what we have to work with?"

I nod. "I get it."

Robyn looks down the pier toward the Ferris wheel. Max is still sweeping, although he's moved closer to the ladybug ride.

"Well, that's the tour," she says. "It isn't much, but it's our world for the summer."

I shrug. "It's very manageable."

She smiles. "You're sweet. She looks up at Max again and adds, "You better go back and help him. Maybe he'll pick up the pace."

"You got it, boss."

"I don't know why I thought this year would be any different," Max whines on the walk to my house after work. "Each year she gives me the same crappy jobs. Sweep the deck, mop the deck, clear the trash bins, scrape off the bird poop. It sucks! I don't know why she's singling me out."

"Aren't you one of the cleaners?"

"Well yeah, but it seems like she's always picking on *me*. Never Mackenzie. Never Carl. Always me."

"But you've been there longer than anyone else, right?" We stop at the corner of Third Street and Montana Boulevard and wait until it's clear to cross.

"I mean, I guess so. I don't know. Still seems to me like she's on a power trip this year."

I stare down at the cracked sidewalk as we get closer to Cemetery Street. "You *were* kind of giving her attitude this morning when I came in."

"Who's side are you on, man? Are you defending her?"

"No—I mean—I'm just saying, I can see where she's coming from. But look, today was my first day, so I don't know what I'm saying."

"Well, you don't know her like the rest of us," he says. "She can be nasty."

I doubt that, but I keep my mouth shut. Max and Peggy have both already made it clear that most people

<h1>Summer Job</h1>

at the Pier don't like Robyn. If I want to keep the peace with them—especially if Max becomes my roommate—I need to tread carefully. Still, I think it's unfair the way they're completely writing off Robyn so early in the season. She seemed really nice to me.

And I'm standing by my cute comment.

My house sits right next to the old motel in town. There's a long wooden fence along the property line that's overgrown with weeds and vines, but at least it's better than staring at a cracked, forgotten parking lot. The house is a small bungalow with a wide front porch and a peaked roof. It's actually in very good condition for being a rental.

"Oh wow, this place *is* nice," Max says as we approach. "I thought when you said it was nice earlier that you meant there were no bugs, but this is a *house*."

I pull my keys out of my pocket with a grin. "Yeah, it's pretty sweet."

"How'd you get ahold of this?"

"It was in the paper."

"Fair enough."

I unlock the door and step into the open great room that serves as the living room, kitchen, and dining room all in one. Through the kitchen, there's a door that leads to a covered back porch. To the left is the hallway leading to the two bedrooms and the bathroom. The ceilings are vaulted to the roof with a loft space over the bedrooms.

"Damn, dude, this is nice!" Max steps inside with his mouth hanging open and wide eyes.

I chuckle. "You already said that."

"But I mean it."

There's a beat-up love seat against one wall and my grandmother's old rocking chair in the corner, both pointed at the TV. There are three barstools by the counter that were there when I moved in.

"I guess the landlord just finished a renovation. The yard is still kind of a mess in the back. The pool is all murky, so I wouldn't go in there, but the house is nice." I watch as he moves into the kitchen and looks out the back window. I point to the hallway to the left of the front of the house. "The bedrooms are through there. Yours would be the one in the back."

He steps around the corner into the empty second bedroom. "Decent size. Much bigger than my room now."

"Just as long as it's not a mess by time we move out at the end of the summer."

He looks over at me. "You're not staying?"

I shake my head. "Not unless I find a job down here."

"Which is unlikely."

I shrug. "It could happen."

Summer Job

"In your dreams."

"Well, it's a month-to-month lease, so we can see where we're at later. But what do you say? Does this work for you?"

He laughs and shakes my hand. "Yeah, man. This works for me. When can I move in?"

Chapter Three:
ROBYN

I take a sip of my crappy home-brewed coffee as I make my way down First Street. It's opening day for the Pier and it's early. The sun is just rising over the ocean and I can see the silhouette of my best friend Jessie running on the beach.

She and her grandma run Montana Manor, which is the only inn in town. She always wakes up super early to run and I admire her for it, but I don't have time for that. I have things to do and places to be. Besides, I work on my feet most of the day. I get my exercise in.

The coffee shop is just opening up when I walk by. I wave to Nancy through the window, but keep on walking. I don't have time to stop. I didn't even work on my painting at all this morning. I'm too focused on the

Summer Job

Pier today. It's taken some nagging, but my team and I finally got it all cleaned up and ready for customers this past week. Still, there's some office work that I need to do before the day gets started, so I want to get there early.

At the office, I flick on the light and hit the power button for the computer. Spinning in my chair, I check the schedule for today on the cork board behind my desk as I wait for it to warm up. Peggy and Max are both working today. Not my favorite, but Peggy needs to be here because she's my assistant and it's opening day and, whether I like it or not, Max has been here the longest, which means I can count on him to get things done.

When he shows up.

I notice that Jaden is also working today. I had Mackenzie show him how to run the rides and no matter what ride I put him on, he seemed to pick it up right away. Plus, he's been a big help this past week with everything else. I'm curious to see how he and the other new people do now that the park's open.

Once the computer is up and running, I look at some of the stats from the last several years. Slowly, the numbers on opening day are decreasing, although the money made each season has increased. Rising ticket prices and more money spent at concessions helped with that. Not to mention, we got a fairly-popular comedian from North Beach to come and do a show here last summer, which drew a large crowd. He was booked already for this year, so we won't have him. We have half the season booked, but no one as popular as he was.

I crunch some numbers and figure we'll have to have even more people this year than last year if we want to meet our financial goals. I don't like trying to estimate concession sales because that's usually pretty dependent on the weather. If it's really sunny, more people buy drinks. If it's cloudy, less drinks sold. I guess the same can be said about ticket sales, though.

The business is still profitable, but not by a lot. Nobody's getting rich off the Montana Beach Pier. It makes me wonder how many more years we'll be open. If the owner decides his money is better spent elsewhere, we're stuck because nobody who truly cares for the Pier has enough to keep it open. We just need to keep things going for as long as possible.

"Am I too early?"

I jump and bump my coffee. It spills all over my desk onto the floor.

"I'm sorry!" Jaden rushes forward to help me move the papers away. "I didn't mean to scare you."

"It's okay," I mutter. "I must've been zoning out. Here, let me get some paper towels." I hurry into the break room and grab the whole roll.

He holds up some of the soggy papers from my desk. "I hope none of this was too important."

I rip off several sheets from the roll and start wiping up the floor. "Nothing that can't be printed again, I suppose."

"What is all this stuff?" he asks, patting at the papers with a wad of paper towels.

"Just some attendance projections."

"Like customers?"

"Yeah."

"Does it sound promising?"

I shrug.

"Oh."

I glance up at him and toss the soiled paper towels in the trash. "Not horrible. You're not going to find yourself unemployed in the middle of the summer, but things could be better."

"I see, yeah. I was talking to Max the other day and he said that the Pier is actually one of the only attractions left in Montana Beach." He wipes up what's left of the coffee from the desk.

"Besides the beach," I add. I'm surprised that Max would give any sort of compliment to this place, but then, there has to be a reason he keeps coming back. He can't hate it here — or me — *that* much.

"That's kind of sad," Jaden says. "It's nice here."

With the floor wiped up, I take my seat again and help him dab at the papers. "Well, I'm glad you like it. Have you been exploring the town much?"

"Not really because we've been working so much. I went to the beach the other day when I had off. It's quiet. I liked it."

"That's good. Yeah, sorry about having you jump in full time right away. We kind of need all hands on deck at the start of the season."

"No worries." He tosses more wet paper towels in the trash and gathers the dried papers. "So this place really isn't doing too hot?"

"I'm probably just overreacting." I try to downplay it. It's probably not a good idea to get the employees worried. "Don't go spreading it around that things are bad."

He takes a seat in the chair across from me and shakes his head. "I won't. Is there anything I can do to help?"

"You mean *not* make me spill my coffee?" I smirk.

His face darkens a little. "Sorry again."

"Don't worry about it. But as far as what you can do, really the biggest thing is to just help keep the rest of the staff in line. Everyone hates me because I'm the only one calling them out for being lazy. The last manager just let everyone do whatever. That's probably why he got fired. Anyway, since I've been promoted, they haven't liked me."

He scratches behind his ear and looks at the floor. "Yeah, I kind of got that impression."

I open my mouth to respond, but I hear the door open into the break room and Peggy steps in.

"I'll go out and start sweeping," Jaden says quickly.

"Good idea. Thanks."

He's out the door before Peggy comes into the office.

To my surprise, there are more customers at the Pier than I thought there would be. The only real hiccup to the day is having to cover for Max's tardiness. He finally strolled in half an hour after we opened, which was a full hour after he was scheduled to be here. Luckily, since he's a cleaner, there wasn't a lot to clean first thing in the morning, but I'm still not happy about it. But, if that's the only real issue on opening day, I'm a good with that. It's not like I wasn't expecting it anyway.

By the time I check the day's numbers at closing, I'm very happy to see that there were more people this year than last year. It's always hard to tell what marketing efforts helped bring more people through the doors, but I'll definitely have to do some investigating tomorrow.

I count out the day's money and enter it into the computer separated by concessions and ticket sales. By the time I'm done, I have a big pile of cash sitting on the desk that needs to be verified by someone else, but everyone's cleared out for the day. After the sound of kids giggling and screaming all day long, it's weird for there to be complete silence in the office.

Peggy's supposed to stay with me to help me close, but she took off early because her son had a doctor's appointment. Valid excuse, I suppose. I just wish she had scheduled it for another day, but I guess you can't always choose.

I was so busy in the shuffle that I forgot to ask Max to stay. Besides Peggy, he's the next logical choice to help me count out the day's money and make sure the Pier is in tip-top shape for tomorrow's opening. Based purely on seniority, obviously. He took off as soon as seven o'clock hit and the park officially closed. Wouldn't want to spend an extra minute here.

I look out the window and see Jaden putting a garbage bag in one of the cans by the gates. I'm surprised he's still here since everyone else went home. Either way, I'm glad he is because now I can close out everything tonight instead of rushing through it tomorrow morning.

I pop my head out the door and ask, "Hey, can you come in here and help me for a sec?"

"Uh, sure." He follows me into the office and takes a seat across from the desk. "I know my shift ended at seven, and if you don't want to pay me for the time after, I understand. I just wanted to get a few extra things done before I left. I figured it'd be less to do tomorrow."

I smile. "No, that's fine. Actually, I was really happy to see that. Thanks." Hopefully his work ethic will rub off on the rest of the workers.

"No problem," he says. "Just doing my part."

"Well, thank you." I sit back and smile at him. He's so nice and his smile makes me do the same and I could just—

"So…what did you need help with?" he asks.

"Oh!" I grab the wad of cash and pause. "How good are you at counting money?"

"Well, I've had some retail experience—"

"Oh, right! Well, I just need you to count this so we can verify the amount and I can close everything out for tonight." I set the stack on the desk in front of him and pass him a calculator. "I'm sure you've done this before, but I like to count out each hundred and then add that in the calculator, but you can do whatever method works for you. As long as we get the same number, it doesn't really matter." I turn back to the computer and click around, trying to pretend that I wasn't just staring at him.

"Sure thing." He grabs the bills and counts it out quick, like someone who's worked with cash before.

When he's done, he tells me the total, which matches mine, and I plug it into the computer to finish closing everything for the day.

"You can go if you want," I tell him as I stuff the money into the deposit bag. "I'm sure you're getting hungry."

He shakes his head. "No, that's okay. I wouldn't feel comfortable leaving you to walk home alone. It's a small town, but you never know."

I bite my top lip to try to hide my smile, but I probably just come off as a freak. Eh, what else is new? Everyone here hates me already anyway.

Well, everyone except for Jaden.

Once I've finished everything and have turned the computer off, I grab my bag and lead Jaden out of the building, making sure to lock the door behind us.

"Thanks again for all your hard work," I say as we start walking down Ocean Boulevard. "Not just today, but all week. Someone like you is just what we needed around here."

"No problem, ma'am, just—"

Summer Job

I stop walking and grab his arm. "Okay, first of all, don't call me *ma'am*. I'm probably not that much older than you. I may be your boss, but I'm not your mother. Just call me Robyn."

He looks scared and nods quickly.

I laugh. "Sorry, but it just sounded weird. No, definitely call me Robyn."

"Okay." He nods again and then adds, "Robyn."

I start walking again. "Just keep saying it. You'll get used to it."

He chuckles. "Okay, Robyn."

"You said you live on Cemetery Street?"

"Yup. Hey, you remembered."

"Well, after forgetting so much of your history, I'm determined to remember *something*." We turn onto Third Street.

"So you remembered where I live? That seems…creepy." He smiles to show he's joking.

"It's a small town, everyone knows everyone's secrets here. Especially the newbies."

"Guess I better get used to it, then."

"So how was your first day?" I ask. "Well, your first day with the park opened."

Jaden lets out a deep breath. "Busy, just like everyone said it would be."

I chuckle. "Ready for another tomorrow?"

"I need a good night's sleep. Between the sun and being on my feet, I'm wiped."

"Yeah, it can be tiring, but that's part of the reason I love it," I say. "You'll get used to it, too."

"Yeah."

We're quiet as we cross over Montana Boulevard and I turn right, toward Fourth Street—my street.

"How has everyone been treating you?" I ask him.

"Good. They all seem nice, for the most part."

"Don't let them see you with me, then." I laugh.

"Yeah, they definitely don't like you."

"No need to sugarcoat it, then!"

He smiles. "Sorry, but you even said it yourself."

"Yeah," I say with a sigh. "And I don't care *that* much if they like me, I just wish they would respect me and they don't. I mean, look at the way Max was late today. The gates were open before he got there. He's supposed to be there half an hour before we open to get everything in order."

"But what kind of consequence is there for coming in late?" Jaden asks. "Maybe nobody's really afraid of being late because they know nothing's going to happen. They just think you're annoying."

"Oh, thanks!" We turn onto my street.

He chuckles. "I'm just saying, there needs to be consequences when people break the rules."

I nod. "Well, I've been thinking about implementing a point system that tallies up when people are late, but I haven't really fleshed out the details yet."

"So do it. There will be growing pains, of course, but you need to make them afraid of you a little bit."

"Yeah, maybe. I'll come up with something." I slow down in front of my house. "This is me."

It's a little two-story house. Blue, like a lot of the houses in town, with white trim work. There's a palm tree in the front yard near the white picket fence that has chipped paint and there's a small flower garden under the bay window in the front of the house. The porch swing sways in the slight breeze by the red front door.

He nods. "Nice place."

"Thanks. And thanks for walking me home." I look down at the broken sidewalk and then up at the house. "Well, I guess I'll see you tomorrow, then."

"Yeah, definitely," he says. "I can even stay late again if you want."

"That'd be nice, yeah. You definitely counted the money faster than Peggy."

"It's not hard."

"No, it's not." I shove my hands in my pockets. "Well, good night."

"Night." He slowly turns and continues down the

street. I watch him until he reaches the end and turns right.

What is it about that boy that makes me want to linger like this?

More by the Author

To find more books by the author, visit
DavidNethBooks.com/Books

* * *

Subscribe to his newsletter to be the first to know of new releases and special deals!
DavidNethBooks.com/Newsletter

* * *

If you enjoyed the book, please consider leaving a review on Goodreads or the retailer you bought it from. Reviews help potential readers determine whether they'll enjoy a book, so any comments on what you thought of the story would be very helpful!

About the Author

D. Allen is the author of the sweet small town romance series, Montana Beach and Small Town Christmas.

Also writes fantasy and superhero fiction as David Neth.

www.DavidNethBooks.com
www.facebook.com/DavidNethBooks

www.ingramcontent.com/pod-product-compliance
Lightning Source LLC
Chambersburg PA
CBHW030749190726
48285CB00003B/770